Wagons Roll

Grizzly Smalls, a scout during the Indian wars, has a premonition of danger when he discovers that some of the Lakota Sioux are on the warpath again. He informs Ben Nolan, but Ben has troubles of his own. He is on the trail of a consignment of rifles which have been stolen by outlaws, and the attractive Dora is moving out of his life with the wagon train heading for the Indian territories.

Grizzly's prediction of gun fights comes true when the wagon train is attacked by the Indians. Can Ben arrive in time to save Dora and prevent the guns from falling into the wrong hands?

Wagons Roll

Ted Rushgrove

A Black Horse Western

ROBERT HALE · LONDON

© Ted Rushgrove 2006
First published in Great Britain 2006

ISBN-10: 0-7090-8139-1
ISBN-13: 978-0-7090-8139-5

Robert Hale Limited
Clerkenwell House
Clerkenwell Green
London EC1R 0HT

Typeset by
Derek Doyle & Associates, Shaw Heath
Printed and bound in Great Britain by
Antony Rowe Limited, Wiltshire

CHAPTER 1

Wayne Peters, the train driver, blew his whistle as the train approached the bend. This section of the line ran largely across the prairie, but now they were nearing some foothills. In fact the line had been as straight as an arrow for eighteen miles. Wayne knew the exact lay-out of the track since he had driven the train over it for the past two years – ever since the line had been opened in fact.

For good measure he gave another blast on his whistle. Not that he expected to find anything unusual round the corner. The days when the buffaloes roamed the prairie were gone several years back. The government had paid the buffalo hunters five dollars a head to kill them, in order to force the Indians to leave the prairie to the settlers. He had never agreed with that policy. After all, the Indians were here first. Surely the country was big enough for everybody. But it had meant the disappearance of the buffaloes – which in turn meant that there were no wild animals for him to be concerned about being hit by the train. There were coyotes and foxes of course, but in their way they were both crafty animals and saw to it that they kept away from the train.

Sometimes he even wished he could see an animal or two to break the monotony of the run. There was an occasion just after the line was opened when they had had that hard winter and he had been surprised by what he saw – it was a bear. In fact five or six – a whole family of them. That had been a rare sight. He wished he had had one of those newfangled cameras to record it for his children. And maybe eventually his grandchildren. Thinking of his family brought his thoughts neatly round to the fact that he would be with his family in less than an hour. The train was due to arrive in Carlton at four o'clock. Usually they were anything from ten minutes to half an hour late and, on one occasion, as much as two hours, but people didn't mind. This was the West and the hustle and bustle of the big towns hadn't really come here yet. He had no doubt that it would, but at present people could take their time. They could even say 'hullo' to one other when they met in the streets – a practice which he heard had died out in the big towns.

His thoughts were interrupted by the fact that the train was now on the bend. He had, of course, slowed down. He gave another blast on his whistle. It was a gradual bend which meant that he couldn't see what was around the corner for several seconds. He had automatically taken up his position with his head out through the cabin so that he would be able to see what was around the corner as soon as possible. On this occasion his face registered shock and disbelief when he was able to see the line ahead clearly. Barely a hundred yards away the line was blocked by large boulders.

His reaction was automatic. He jammed on the brakes. The wheels screamed their protest as they released showers of sparks. Wayne knew that the people in the train would have been hurled around by the sudden change in movement from the normal steady progress to the horrendous attempt to stop before the train hit the boulders.

Wayne's whole attention was concentrated on them. They were coming frighteningly near by the second. He couldn't even contemplate what would happen if the train did hit them. How far away were they now? A couple of hundred yards? Less than that? He found that he was automatically gripping the handle. There was nothing he could do. He was overwhelmed by his own helplessness. It was in the hands of God whether the brakes would stop the train before it reached the boulders.

'Do you think we will stop?'

For a second he thought that his mind was playing tricks on him and that he had actually heard the thought which was hammering through his mind. Then he realized that it was his fireman, Stan Davey. He, too, was staring at the deadly, fascinating boulders as they approached them.

The train was definitely slowing. He tried to calculate its speed as if it were approaching a station. How far were the boulders? A hundred yards?

The train was definitely coming to a halt. Its speed had now dropped to a crawl. Wayne quickly calculated that even if they hit the boulders at this speed it shouldn't be enough to derail them. The boulders were now only about twenty yards away. The train came to a shuddering halt.

'Thank God!' Wayne cried aloud in relief.

'We've done it.' The excitement was shared by Stan.

Their relief, however, was short-lived. Half-a-dozen riders had appeared from behind a nearby bluff. The masks they wore over their faces denoted their particular line of business. Wayne rightly assumed that they were the ones who had been responsible for blocking the line.

CHAPTER 2

In the Red Garter saloon in Carlton, Grizzly Smalls was recounting a story. That in itself was not an unusual event since Grizzly had a wealth of stories. He had collected them during his fifty years in a variety of occupations.

'Did I ever tell you how I escaped from the Injuns when they were about to slit my throat from ear to ear?' he demanded.

Some of the regulars who had heard the story before wandered away from the corner of the saloon where he habitually sat. However a few stayed to listen.

'Of course, telling a story is always thirsty work,' said Grizzly, slyly.

One of the listeners took the hint. He relieved Grizzly of his empty tankard and had it refilled at the bar.

'Thank you kindly, sir,' said Grizzly, as he accepted it. He half-emptied the tankard in one swallow before going ahead with his story.

'If any of you think that the Injun wars ended on one particular day, you are wrong,' he began. 'They went on for at least a couple of years after the government said that they were all over. Of course the government said that so that all the politicians could get re-elected. I've never had any truck with politicians.' He spat unerringly into a spittoon to emphasize his point.

'This particular time I was trapping in Injun country – or at least what had been Injun country a couple of years hack. I'd got a nice collection of furs – foxes and beavers, but some of them were silver foxes and I knew I could get a good price for them in Herford. In fact I was packing up the furs and carrying them to the canoe ready to go back down river towards civilization when he appeared.'

Grizzly paused dramatically.

'The Indian?' demanded one of the listeners.

'No, the bear,' stated Grizzly, dramatically. 'He stood staring at me. He couldn't have been more than twenty yards away. He was the meanest-looking black bear that you ever saw.'

'What did you do?' demanded another, while Grizzly almost drained his tankard in another swallow.

Grizzly wiped his ample beard. 'There was nothing I could do. My gun was in the tent. I could have dropped my furs and run towards the river, but the chances were I wouldn't have been able to reach it.'

'You don't mean to say that a bear can run faster than you?' demanded one listener, incredulously.

'That's just what I am saying, sonny. Over a couple of hundred yards I wouldn't back any of you here to outrun a bear.'

'But he couldn't have attacked you, since you are here to tell the tale,' suggested another.

'He didn't attack me because the Injun saved my life,' said Grizzly. 'This Injun suddenly appeared. He was an Injun brave and what was unusual about him was that he was wearing war paint.'

'War paint?' enquired one.

'Yes, war paint. I don't know whether any of you have ever seen an Injun wearing war paint?'

There was a concerted shaking of heads.

'They are naked except for a loin cloth. They cover their bodies in a red dye that they get from some tree or other. They use a white dye on part of their faces together with the red dye. They wear eagle-feathers in their hair. They've got a tomahawk in their belts and they carry a spear that's dripping with blood – from some animal or other they've killed. The sight of them is enough to scare the living daylights out of their enemies.'

'So what happened? Did he scare you?'

'No. But he scared the bear.'

There was a general chorus of disbelief.

'I'm telling you as true as I'm standing here. The bear took one look at the Injun, and turned and trotted off.'

'So what happened next?'

'Well the Injun had saved my life. He said he'd come to kill me to avenge all the killings done by the white folk, but when he saw that I could speak his own language we became quite friendly. Especially when I gave him some of my furs for saving my life.'

'It's a good story, but I don't believe it,' said one.

'In exchange for my furs he gave me this,' said Grizzly. He reached in his pouch and produced an unusual object.

'It's a scalp,' said the disbeliever, recoiling hastily.

Grizzly began to laugh. In fact he laughed so much that when one of the listeners asked him whether wanted another drink, he was unable to speak. However, by his gesture towards the bar the person rightly assumed that he meant yes.

Unnoticed by Grizzly, two well-dressed men had been seated not far way. They were near enough to have heard his story.

'He's our man,' said one.

The other nodded in agreement.

CHAPTER 3

The meeting started as usual with prayers. After the preacher had prayed for the good health and continued faith of the members he came to the part of his prayers which was on everybody's mind.

'. . . and may our venture, O Lord, be crowned with success. We will be going into unknown territory. We will face all kinds of dangers. Our faith may even be sorely tried. Some of us have doubts about the wisdom of this venture. But I am sure that with your guidance, in the end, we will overcome all obstacles.' He concluded with the Lord's Prayer, in which they all joined him.

While coffee and cookies were being served by the ladies there was a constant hubbub of conversation.

'When do you think we'll be starting?' The question was repeated several times. Each time the preacher, a red-faced, sturdy man who looked more like a farmer than a preacher, gave the same answer.

'We hope to start moving shortly. Most of the arrangements have been made but there are one or two problems still outstanding.'

His assistant, Mrs Timms, a slight woman, who was never far from his side, would usually add to his statement.

'We'll put a notice here in the hall to notify you of the exact date when we know it.'

A matronly woman who had a couple of small children clinging to her skirt, demanded, 'Are you sure there will be enough provision made for the children?'

This time Mrs Timms herself answered the question. 'The children will be well cared for, Emma. As you know Miss Rowe will be in charge of them. She's been a very good Sunday-school teacher. I'm sure she'll continue to be just as dependable in the future.'

As if on cue, Miss Rowe handed Mrs Timms a cup of coffee. She was a very attractive young lady. So much so that several of the other ladies in the congregation often regarded her with envy and wondered why she had so far not achieved the ultimate aim of most women – marriageable status.

'I will look after the children, Mrs Timms,' she

said, with assurance.

A short while later the preacher clapped his hands.

'If everyone has finished their refreshments then I declare the meeting closed. It only remains to thank you all for coming. Will Paul Middleton and Harry Cranshaw stay behind? There are a few matters which we have to discuss.'

The congregation trooped out slowly. The two men who stayed behind were, like the preacher, both middle-aged.

They sat near the front of the hall.

'Any last-minute problems, Sam?' demanded Harry. He was a tall man – well over six feet in height. He had been the preacher's right-hand man for several years, although he had always avoided being officially called a curate.

'If there are we'll have to know about them now,' voiced Paul. He was a short man who often spent time in Harry's company. So much so in fact that Harry's wife, Sally, sometimes had to drop pertinent hints that it was their bedtime when Paul gave every sign of staying in their house late in the evening.

Sam sat in a chair facing them. 'It's about the wagon train leader.'

'What about him?' demanded Harry.

'As you know there hasn't been a wagon train

for years in this part of the territory. So we hired those two agents to find a leader for us—'

'Don't say they haven't been able to fmd anybody,' stated Paul.

'Oh, they've found somebody. He's – quite old.'

'He would be,' affirmed Harry. 'Since there haven't been any wagon trains for years.'

'He says that he will take us.'

'What's this guy's name?' demanded Paul.

'Grizzly Smalls.'

'That's an unusual name,' said Harry.

'At one time he was a trapper. He claims that he even caught a bear. Hence his name.'

'So we've got a wagon train leader who obviously knows the locality,' said Paul. 'What's the problem?'

Sam hesitated before replying. At last he said: 'He drinks.'

'You mean he's a drunkard?' demanded Harry.

'No, I don't think so. At least the two agents said that he wasn't one. It's just that he's a regular drinker in the saloon.'

'Of course, it goes against all our principles,' stated Harry.

'I think in this case we'll have to shelve our no-drinking rule,' said Sam.

'We haven't got any other choice, have we?' demanded Paul.

'No. It seems that there aren't many wagon train leaders left. So we've got to take what we can. That means accepting Grizzly Smalls. Do you agree?'

They both raised their hands in agreement.

CHAPTER 4

In the Pinkerton office in Chicago, Burke, the deputy director, had a worried frown on his face. He was a heavy-featured middle-aged man who was not particularly handsome and the frown did nothing to enhance his appearance. His assistant, Grey, regarded his boss's face apprehensively. Burke was known for his fiery temper and on the occasions when Grey had been a witness to these outbursts he had noted that they had usually been preceded by a frown. The kind of frown that was now on Burke's face.

'You've seen this, I suppose?' Burke flung a newspaper on to his desk. Grey reached across to retrieve it.

On the front page was a description of the recent hold-up of the train on its way to Carlton. Grey had already read the report, but he re-read it slowly, hoping it would give time for his boss's expression to change. When he eventually looked up he saw that his assumption was mistaken. Burke's face looked as forbidding as before.

'It's a bad business,' said Grey, realizing that it was up to him to make the opening comment.

'It's a bad business. It's a bloody tragic business.' Burke was shouting. Grey wondered whether they would be able to hear him in the adjoining offices.

'Luckily nobody was killed,' ventured Grey.

'That's not the point.' Burke picked up the newspaper, rolled it up and banged his desk with it.

'Except of course the train driver, who sprained his ankle when the outlaws told him to jump down from the cabin.'

'Are you stupid, Grey?'

It was obviously a rhetorical question which did not require an answer. Grey wisely kept quiet.

'What was on the train?'

'Guns.'

'Guns. To be exact, rifles. Winchester repeating rifles. Forty-eight of them. Now do you get it?' He stared at Grey like a teacher trying to impress Pythagoras's theorem on a rather backward pupil.

'You mean why should the outlaws want the rifles?'

19

'That's exactly what I mean. This hold-up was obviously carefully planned. The gang knew the rifles were on the train. They seized them. They did not bother with any of the valuables the passengers were carrying. Which leads us to the question: why would they want forty-eight rifles?'

'To use themselves in their hold-ups?' suggested Grey.

'Yes, that is a possibility.'

Grey heaved a silent sigh.

'Except for one thing.'

Grey's moment of relief vanished. 'You mean: why should a gang of six outlaws require all those rifles?'

'That's very good, Grey. I can see there's hope for you yet. At last you've got the point.'

Grey was used to his chief's sarcasm. At least it was preferable to his temper outbursts.

'The obvious assumption is that they want to sell most of the guns to somebody else.'

Burke was staring at him. It was the sort of stare that told Grey it was his turn to speak.

'You mean somebody like the Indians?'

'I doubt it. The Indians were a spent force several years ago. Although there are rumours that there are some hotheads who are trying to get a war party together. No, I think we can discount the Indians.'

'Who then?' Grey was genuinely puzzled.

'We don't know the name of this gang. All we know is that it seems that it has six members. Now, just supposing, for the sake of argument, that the leader of the gang decided he would like to recruit more members. How would he recruit them?'

'I don't know. Offer them money?'

'Offer them rifles, Grey. Winchester repeating rifles. The best rifles around. Now if our gang has these rifles it should be easy for them to recruit new members. They could increase their members. The more members they have the more crimes they could commit. The more banks they could rob. The more trains they could hold up.'

'It's not a pretty picture,' stated Grey. He, too, had a frown on his face.

'It's up to us to try to stop it,' continued his chief. 'We've got to give it top priority. I've already sent out five agents to various towns to see whether they can glean any information about the gang.'

'What can I do?' demanded Grey.

'I want you to send telegrams to these sheriffs.' Burke gave him a list. 'Tell them to watch out for any suspicious wagon that has recently arrived in their town. It would have to be a wagon, I doubt whether the outlaws could hide the rifles on anything smaller – like a buggy.'

'I'll get on to it, right away,' said Grey, eager to make his escape.

'If we could catch the outlaws before they do any damage it would be a feather in our cap,' stated Burke.

In your cap, you mean, thought Grey, as he went through the door. If there's any praise to be shared out, Burke saw to it that he would receive one hundred per cent of it.

CHAPTER 5

Grizzly was in his customary seat in his customary corner of the Red Garter saloon. It was a quiet time in the afternoon and apart from a few card-players and a couple of regulars who were standing by the bar talking to the bartender, there was very little activity.

The door swung open and two men came in. They were in their thirties and dressed in dark suits. They spotted Grizzly and went over to him.

'Hullo, Mr Smalls,' said one. 'Do you remember us?'

'I always remember a face,' replied Grizzly. 'Especially when, the last time I saw him, that person bought me a drink.'

The person whom Grizzly had addressed showed no change in facial expression at the blatant invitation to buy a drink. He signalled to his companion to refill Grizzly's tankard.

'Let me see,' said Grizzly reflectively. 'If I remember rightly your name is Mr Latchford and your friend's name is Mr Klint.'

'That's right,' said the other, as he sat and prepared to wait for the drinks to arrive.

Grizzly correctly assumed that it wasn't the right time for casual conversation, so he placed his elbows on the table and waited for the drinks.

When Klint arrived with the drinks Latchford began: 'We've been consulting with certain people – the ones we mentioned when we talked to you a few days ago. The upshot is that they would like you to take charge of the wagon train.'

'Hang on a minute,' said Grizzly. He emptied half his tankard in one swallow. The two seated opposite him weren't sure whether he meant them to hang on while he had the drink or whether it was a conversational request. It was obviously the latter.

'I'll want some more details before I give a definite yes,' said Grizzly.

'We were under the impression that you were quite prepared to lead the wagon train,' said Klint, speaking for the first time.

'So I am, but there are a few questions to be answered first.'

'If you want more money I don't think our

24

clients will be able to find it,' stated Latchford. 'They are poor people who hope to make a living for themselves out West.'

'It's not the money,' said Grizzly. 'Two hundred dollars and all found was the agreed sum. That's OK by me.' He didn't add that it was more than he had earned during the last couple of years just doing odd jobs around the town or for the farmers.

'What's the problem?' demanded Latchford.

'I want to know more about this wagon train. Who are the people I'll be taking West? Why do they want to go? There are no gunslingers among them, are there?'

Latchford permitted himself a smile. He gave the impression of a person who was always in complete control and never did anything in excess.

'We mentioned that they are Christians. They don't have anything to do with guns, let alone gunslingers.'

'How many wagons are there?' demanded Grizzly.

'Eight,' answered Klint.

'That means nine,' said Grizzly.

'Where does the other one come in?' demanded Latchford.

'It's the chuck wagon. Without it the wagon train wouldn't get fifty miles.'

'Yes, well, you're the expert,' said Latchford.

'I'll want to meet the person in charge. I'll want to see the colour of their money.'

'You'll get paid. You don't have to worry about that,' snapped Klint.

It was the first time either man had shown any emotion and Grizzly raised his bushy eyebrows.

'I'll want the money in advance,' said Grizzly, calmly.

'That's up to the committee,' said Latchford.

'I still want to meet them. A few days before they are due to start. There are things they won't know that they will need on the trail.'

'How many days do you think it will take to get to their journey's end?' demanded Klint.

'You can never tell. There could be happenings which will slow the wagon down – a broken wheel, a horse might go lame, or it might be bitten by a rattler . . .'

'How many days roughly do you think it will take,' persisted Klint.

'Roughly, I'd say twenty days to reach the Indian territories. But you could probably add a couple of days on if the weather turns nasty.'

Grizzly drained his tankard. Klint went to the bar for a refill. Neither Grizzly nor Latchford took any notice of the two men who were playing cards at a nearby table. The men stood up and one of them scooped up the few dollars he had won.

One of the men who were left at the table, said:

'Maybe we'll see you here again.'

'Maybe,' said one of the strangers, as he pulled on his gloves.

CHAPTER 6

Ben Nolan sat in the train to Carlton. He was not in a particularly happy frame of mind. Usually he liked a train journey. The novelty of the form of transport, which had only been running for a couple of years, had not yet worn off. He enjoyed mixing with the fellow-travellers – wealthy Americans, their poorer brethren, other nationalities, such as English, French, German, Mexican and others all contributed to a variety of humanity which he enjoyed watching. He liked watching the children with their excited faces as they waited to board the train. Once the train had started it was a pleasure to watch the changing scenery – even the prairie seemed to convey a different impression from a train. But not on this occasion.

It all started when Burke, the deputy director of Pinkertons, had given him the task of going to

Carlton to try to find the missing guns.

'I know it's like searching for a needle in a haystack,' Burke had told him, 'but I'm hoping that you or one of the other detectives will turn up something.'

Burke knew that he was sending him on a hopeless errand. It was a wild-goose chase. The guns had disappeared several days before. The local sheriff hadn't been able to find any clues about the gang who had taken them. True, the train had been held up a short distance outside Carlton, but that didn't mean anything. The guns had been taken off the train and could now be as much as a hundred miles away. They could even be on their way to the Mexican border as far as he knew.

There was another reason for his less than happy mental state – his love-life hadn't worked out as he had hoped. He had hoped that the preacher's daughter, Sylvia, would have married him. In fact everything in the garden had seemed rosy – except for one thing. He had confessed to her that he had had a love-affair with a married woman and as a result she had had a baby. At first Sylvia had seemed to accept the situation and had forgiven him. But as time had passed she kept referring to it regularly. This had eventually got under his skin. They had had a blazing row. The result was they had parted. That was over three months ago. But the fact that they had split up still rankled.

The train eventually reached Carlton. The travellers disembarked. He knew that there was one person to contact before he found somewhere to stay.

The sheriff's office wasn't difficult to find. When Ben went inside he found that the sheriff himself took up a large part of the office. He was a big man. Probably at one time he had been a muscular man, but now the muscle was largely fat.

Ben introduced himself. The sheriff, whose name was Stephens, waved him to a chair. The sheriff's own chair creaked as he moved.

'What can I do for you, Mr Nolan?'

Ben explained how Pinkerton's Agency was trying to trace the rifles which had been stolen when the train had been held up.

'Yes, I've had a telegram from the Agency's chief. He asked me whether I could give him any idea what had happened to the Winchesters. I've had to admit I couldn't help him. The outlaws who carried out the robbery have just vanished, together with the rifles.'

'I agree it's like looking for a needle in a haystack. Especially with nothing to go on.'

'Of course somebody must have known in the first place that the guns were on the train.'

'We've got an agent working on that end of the trail. He's visiting the factory. So far he hasn't come up with anything.'

The sheriff again shifted in his chair and it groaned under his weight. 'All I can say, Mr Nolan, is that we'll watch out for any suspicious characters who've come into the town. As you can see Carlton is a growing town and there are dozens of people coming and going daily. So our chances of success in that respect are probably also very slight.'

At that moment a young lady knocked at the outer door and entered. Ben noted with approval that she was attractive.

'What can I do for you, Miss Rowe?' demanded the sheriff.

'We need your help, Sheriff.' There was more than a note of urgency in her voice. A whole octave in fact.

'What is it? What's the matter?'

'A gunman has taken some of the children hostage. He says he will shoot them unless we agree to let him come with us.'

'I'll come over to the hall as quickly as I can. Unfortunately my deputy is away on an errand.'

Ben registered the disappointment in Miss Rowe's face. It was obvious that the sheriff wasn't the world's fastest mover. It would take him twice as long to arrive at the hall as a slighter man.

'I'll come with you,' said Ben.

'You?' She looked at him for the first time.

'I'm a private law officer.'

'We-ell,' indecision struggled with panic.

'Take Mr Nolan with you. I'll be along directly.'

'Come on, Miss Rowe,' said Ben. 'Show me where the incident is taking place.'

'It's not an incident.' She flared up. 'It could be a tragedy unless it's prevented.'

She led the way at a rapid walk that was almost a run. Even with Ben's long legs he had difficulty in keeping up with her.

They travelled a couple of hundred yards along Main Street, then she suddenly turned down a lane. At the end of it Ben could see a wooden building.

'He's in there. I was taking my Bible class when he burst in. I was about to go into the kitchen to get some refreshment for the children. He had a gun. I had to make a quick decision. I went out through the kitchen door before he could lock it. Maybe I did the wrong thing. Maybe I should have stayed with the children.'

'You did the right thing to get help.'

The wisdom of Ben's statement was open to doubt when there was the sound of a shot and a bullet whistled close to his ear.

His reaction was instantaneous. He flung his

companion down on to the ground and dived down by her side.

'He certainly means business,' Ben observed.

'Is that all you can say?' she hissed. 'There are nine children in there. They were all in my care. I've got to help them.'

She moved as though to stand up. Ben grabbed her arm. 'It won't help the situation if you get yourself shot.'

'What do you suggest that we do, lie here until sunset?'

Ben had been gazing around assessing the situation. While doing so he had drawn his own revolver.

'You're not going to shoot him are you?' she demanded, with alarm.

'Only if I have to. This is what I've got to do. I've got to get near the building.'

'How do you intend to do that? You're the one who could get killed if you try to dash from here to the side of the hall.'

'I've got to try it. It's our only chance. Soon other people will start arriving.'

'Wouldn't it be better if we waited for more help?'

'No. It could mean that more people might get killed.'

Their conversation was interrupted by another bullet. This one landed on the ground not far from them. Miss Rowe instinctively clung close to Ben.

'Right. This is when I go,' said Ben, releasing himself from her hold.

'Take care,' she whispered.

Ben guessed that it was about fifty yards to the building from where they were lying. He took a deep breath. Suddenly he jumped up and started sprinting towards the building.

His move had obviously taken the gunman by surprise. Ben had almost reached the building when bullets began to snap around him. They were all unpleasantly close. One tugged at his sleeve. The main thing though was that he succeeded in reaching the safety of the side of the building.

There were no windows on this side of the building, the windows were obviously on the other side. Ben crept towards the corner where he knew from Miss Rowe's description that there would be another door. Would the gunman chance coming out through that door? It was a possibility, since the gunman might not have noticed that Ben had a gun. When he had run to the safety of the hall he had held the gun down by his side and the gunman might not have spotted it.

However, it was now aimed at the corner of the hall around which the gunman would

34

appear. Ben's slow footsteps ate away the distance to the corner. His nerves were taut as he waited for any unexpected movement. Everything seemed unnaturally silent. Even the birds had stopped singing as though waiting in expectation of some exciting moments ahead.

Ben reached the corner safely. He knew his next move did not guarantee any further safety for him. He had to put his head round the corner to assess the situation there. A head which could be easily blown to pieces if the gunman was standing outside the door.

Whereas a few seconds before everything had been quiet, Ben suddenly heard the sharp cry of a child. It spurred him into action. He stepped round the corner. The gunman was waiting for him. The two guns spat at the same time. Ben knew that his bullet had killed the gunman from the way he fell awkwardly. It took him a few seconds to reassure himself that the gunman's bullet had missed him.

There was a flurry of movement behind him, then suddenly Miss Rowe flew past him.

'Get him out of the way,' she screamed.

Ben obligingly picked up the gunman, having again ascertained that he was indeed dead. He threw him over his shoulder. He was walking back down the lane with his unaccustomed load when the sheriff and another man with a star came walking towards him.

'Is that him?' demanded the sheriff, when Ben unceremoniously dropped the corpse at their feet.

'Yes.'

'I know him,' said the deputy. 'His name is – was – Blight.'

'We'd better get him out of here,' said the sheriff. 'The children will be coming out soon. I don't want them to see him.'

The deputy picked up the corpse.

'You'd better come back to the office,' the sheriff informed Ben. 'I'll want a statement about what exactly happened.'

Twenty minutes later Ben was in the sheriff's office drinking coffee. The corpse had been deposited in an empty cell.

'He spent a lot of his time in the cells,' the deputy explained. 'The doc described him as mentally unstable. He'd be in the cells for petty thieving, molesting women, exposing himself to young children—'

'This is his last visit then,' Ben observed, drily.

'You could say that,' replied the deputy.

Miss Rowe entered. After offering her a seat the sheriff said:

'There'll be no need for you to make a formal statement. Mr Nolan has already made one.'

'I'd like to put it on record that we should

thank Mr Nolan for his appropriate actions, as a result of which the children were probably saved from a longer nightmare of events than actually happened.'

'We'll do that,' confirmed the deputy, as he handed her a cup of coffee.

Ben, who was in the unusual situation of receiving such warm praise, stared at the floor.

'Do you know why Blight appeared in the church hall with a gun?' asked the sheriff.

'He wanted to come with us.' Ben glanced up with interest. 'We're forming a wagon train to go out West,' she explained to Ben, seeing his interest.

'And he wanted to escape too,' said Ben.

'What do you mean, escape? We're not escaping from anything. We're heading for a new land. We're going to have a fresh beginning. It will be a fresh start for everybody. We'll be coming to Canaan.'

Miss Rowe left shortly afterwards.

'You can tell she's a preacher's daughter,' observed the sheriff.

CHAPTER 7

In a remote valley in the hills six men were sheltering. They were the Ossler gang, who had been sheltering there for the past week. Ever since, in fact, they had held up the train.

'When are we going to move, boss?' demanded Filey. He had a sad face with a drooping moustache, but he was the quickest of the gang on the draw and had killed at least half a dozen men.

'I think we may be able to move sooner than we think,' said Ossler. He always wore gloves. He said it was to keep his hands in perfect condition for the times when he chose to follow his passion at the gambling tables. 'You tell them, Hanson.'

The man addressed had a nondescript face. It had been useful when the gang required somebody who could melt into the background whenever there was a crowd.

'The boss and I were playing cards in this saloon in Carlton,' began Hanson, 'where we heard an interesting conversation from the guys at another table. One of the guys said he was taking a wagon train to the West.'

'What's that got to do with us?' demanded Snowy. The reason for the nickname wasn't hard to guess, since his head was crowned by a mop of thick white hair.

'Our problem is that we've got forty-eight Winchester rifles and we cannot move them without attracting attention,' said Ossler.

'We could hire a wagon and take them away,' said one of the twins. His name was Leo and he was only distinguished from his brother by the scar that ran down the side of his face – the result of some fight or other.

'The boss has already explained to us that any wagon that moves will be searched by the lawmen. They've even brought extra men in from the detective agency to check the wagons,' said his twin, Trevor.

'So you think we should join this wagon train to get to Herford?' said Filey.

'It seems the best way to get the guns out of town,' said Ossler.

'Are you sure that the Smith gang are there?' demanded Hanson. 'We wouldn't want to go all the way to Herford and then find that they'd moved on.'

'I had this telegram from them yesterday,' said

Ossler. He held up the telegram. 'It says that they'll stay in town until we turn up.'

'Think of it,' said Filey, rubbing his hands in eager anticipation. 'The Smith gang and us with those brand-new rifles. We could rob any bank in the West.'

'Or rob any train,' suggested Trevor.

'We could even take over a town,' suggested Leo. 'How many are there in the Smith gang?'

'I think they were six the last time I heard,' said Ossler.

There was silence while they considered the idea. It was broken by Snowy.

'If it's the wagon train I heard about when I was in town, it's being run by a lot of religious people.'

'There can only be one wagon train,' said Ossler. 'If they're a group of religious people it shouldn't make any difference. It only means that you lot will have to stop swearing while we're with the wagon train.'

'I'll be damned if I give up swearing,' said Leo, who considered himself the joker of the gang. The others laughed.

'Now we'll want two of you to go into town to find out more about this wagon train,' said Ossler.

'How about me and Leo?' said Trevor. 'You've all been into town so far except us.'

40

'That sounds all right,' said Ossler. 'Remember you two are supposed to be a couple of religious guys. Oh, and see if you can find out anything about the agent from Pinkerton's.'

'What agent?' demanded Snowy.

'When I went to the telegraph office some people who were waiting were talking about a Pinkerton agent who had saved some of the children from a nutter who was holding the children hostage.'

'What did he do?'

'He shot the guy. So see if you can find out anything about him while you are in town, Keep your ears to the ground.'

'It should be easy for him,' said Leo. 'He's got big ears anyhow.'

His brother aimed a friendly kick at him as they stood up to leave the group.

CHAPTER 8

Ben had been invited to tea with Miss Rowe and her father. Ben was rather reluctant to accept the invitation, but he couldn't very well refuse.

Miss Rowe greeted him by the door. Ben noted with approval that she was wearing a dark dress which accentuated her slim figure. He presented her with a bouquet of flowers.

'Beautiful flowers for a beautiful lady.'

'They're lovely,' she said, with a delighted smile.

Inside the house Ben was introduced to her father. Ben formed the impression that he looked more like a farmer than a preacher. He also had a firm handshake which Ben found encouraging.

When they were seated, the preacher began.

'I hope you drink tea, Mr Nolan.'

'Call me Ben. Yes, I don't mind tea.'

'Thank you. My name is Sam. Having afternoon tea is a tradition we brought from the old country.'

'You weren't born in America then?'

'No, we came here about twenty years ago. Of course my wife was alive then. Unfortunately she died shortly after we landed in this country.'

'I'm sorry,' said Ben. 'So your daughter was very young at the time?'

'Yes, Dora was only just over a year old when we sailed from Liverpool. We wanted to get away from the religious bigotry.'

At that moment Dora came in from the kitchen. She began to lay the table.

'I'm afraid you'll have to take us as you see us, Mr Nolan—'

'Ben, please.'

'I'm Dora.' She held out her hand and they shook hands formally.

'I'm sure, Ben, being a man of the world, realizes that we have dispensed with the services of a maid,' said Sam.

Dora brought in a variety of freshly made cakes. Before they started the meal the preacher said grace.

When he had finished, Dora told Ben to help himself.

He was soon enjoying some of the best home-made cakes he had eaten for ages.

43

'Dora's a good cook,' said her father proudly.

'She's an excellent cook,' Ben concurred.

Dora coloured slightly.

After the meal, while Dora was clearing the dishes in the kitchen, Sam asked : 'How did you become a lawman, Ben?'

'Father, you shouldn't ask a guest such questions,' said Dora reproachfully, from the kitchen.

'Oh, I wasn't always a lawman. I've only been a Pinkerton agent for the last couple of years. Before that I had a variety of jobs. At one time I worked in a circus.'

'What did you do?' The question came from Dora, who had come out of the kitchen.

'I threw knives.'

She regarded him with new-found interest.

'Were you a good knife-thrower?'

'I think so. I worked there for a year. I never scratched the lady I was throwing at.'

'What was her name?'

'Marie. She was half-French.'

While the two men were enjoying a smoke Ben entertained Dora and her father by recounting some of the lighter episodes of his life in the circus. Dora was seated on the floor and the glow from the fire reflected in her fair hair.

'It sounds as though there was never a dull moment in circus life,' she observed.

'Yes, it was quite a good life, but like most good things it came to an end.'

'That's a cynical view of life, Ben,' stated Dora.

'Well, maybe.'

Her father excused himself. 'At about this time in the evening I always take a stroll in the garden. For a little prayer and meditation.'

When he had gone Dora said, 'He blames himself for Mother's death.'

'Why should he do that?'

'He thinks that if he hadn't brought us over here she wouldn't have contracted influenza and died.'

'There's the same chance that she might have contracted influenza in England.'

'Scotland, Ben. We came from Scotland.'

'Is that why you're going on the wagon train?'

'How do you mean?'

'Could it be that your father is still trying to avoid the truth about your mother's death by running further away from it? I'm sorry. It's none of my business.'

'You're quite right. It isn't any of your business,' she said, icily.

The preacher noticed the coolness in their relationship when he returned.

'You haven't been telling Ben about the hard times we had back in Scotland, have you?' he demanded half-jokingly.

'No, we've just been having a frank discussion,' she said.

Shortly afterwards Ben excused himself. 'I've had a lovely evening,' he said, truthfully.

'Come again,' said Sam. 'Although you'll have to make it in the next few days. We hope to leave before the end of the week.'

Dora came to the door to see him off.

'In case we don't meet again, thank you for coming to tea. My father enjoyed your company. I don't think I've seen him so relaxed for a long while. He's got a lot on his mind.'

'And you?'

'I found the evening – different from what I expected.'

She held out her hand. Ben took it. She presented a very desirable picture as she stood there framed in the doorway. On impulse Ben drew her towards him. He kissed her.

When she drew away she said: 'That too, wasn't what I expected.'

CHAPTER 9

Later that evening Ben was standing in the bar of the Red Garter saloon. He was a regular evening visitor to the bar on account of the fact that he was one of the residents of the saloon. He would have preferred to have stayed in one of the hotels in the town. But Pinkerton's only allowed him a small allowance for his stay in the town. Due to this parsimony he was forced to choose a saloon. He supposed it was the Scottish blood in the founder of the detective firm which forced him to choose a saloon rather than a hotel in which to stay.

Thinking of Scotland naturally drew his thoughts to Dora. Tall, lissom Dora. Dora of the pretty face and fair hair. Fate had thrown them together on two occasions – literally in the one case, since they had both ended up on the ground while the gunman was holding the children hostage. On the other occasion he had been equally near her when he had kissed her. He didn't know what had possessed him to kiss her instead of just shaking her hand. It had been an instinctive reaction. A pleasant reaction as he recollected. Well, there was one thing for sure – the pleasant moment would not be repeated. As her father had said, they were due to set off in a few days' time – while he was destined to kick his heels in Carlton.

Some time later he was idly watching some card-players. In fact he was debating whether to have another drink or not. He was not a heavy drinker and the debate with himself had come out in favour of his just finishing the beer that was in his glass and turning in for the night. At that moment his attention was drawn to two men who were standing further along the bar. There was something about them that he couldn't quite place. Had he seen them before?

He racked his brains. They were obviously identical twins. Even though they were wearing different-coloured shirts and the one had his hair cut short – maybe to try to establish his iden-tity as different from his brother's The other thing that distinguished him, of course, was the fact that he had a scar down the side of his face. Where had he seen them before? Or maybe he hadn't seen them. Yes, that was it. He grasped at the idea excitedly. Maybe he had seen them in the outlaw room in Pinkerton's.

The outlaw room was distinctive. On the walls were the drawings of outlaws known to Pinkerton's. One of the constant exercises that the agency insisted upon was that any of the agents who were temporarily unemployed and who as a result were forced to stay in the offices for any length of time should spend some of that time in the outlaw room. He himself had spent hours staring at the couple of hundred faces on the walls in the outlaw room.

The more he thought about it, the more convinced he was that he had seen the twins' faces on one of the walls. What were their names? He inched surreptitiously closer to try to catch a little of their conversation. Suddenly he was near enough to hear the one twin address the other as Leo. That was it! The twin with the scar was Leo and the other was Trevor.

Any chances of keeping the element of surprise on his side were dispelled when the barman asked: 'Do you want another drink, Mr Nolan?'

Ben hadn't realized that in his quest for the truth about the identities of the outlaws he had emptied his glass.

'Nolan!' echoed one of the twins. They spun round instantly to face him.

Ben realized that his time was almost up. The fact that there were two of them and only one of him made the outcome of the inevitable gunfight a foregone conclusion. He knew he could take one. It didn't really matter which one. Because as sure as night follows day the other would get him before he would be able to fire at him.

Silence had descended on the bar – the way it always did when the watchers were about to view a gunfight. Several of them moved purposefully out of range of the expected bullets. For a mad moment Ben thought about denying that he was Nolan. Then he instantly rejected the idea. He would go down in annals of Pinkerton's as just another agent who had died in the line of duty.

The twins had moved so that there was a gap of a few feet between them. This cut down even further his chances of getting the two of them – since he would have to adjust his aim to cover the distance between them – a near impossibility in the split second in which he would have to fire his second shot.

These thoughts flashed through his mind as he automatically took up his position.

'If I remember rightly you two are Leo and Trevor. You are both outlaws who are wanted for murder and robbery.'

'You might have a good memory, lawman,'

snapped Leo. 'But it won't do you any good because you'll be pushing up the daisies in a few seconds.'

'Which one will I take?' demanded Ben. 'You, Trevor? Are you afraid to die?'

'Don't listen to him,' shouted Leo. 'He's trying to get you riled so that it will put you off your shot.'

'You know I can take either one of you,' persisted Ben. 'I'm just giving you the choice.'

His words had an electrifying effect. The two outlaws went for their guns. Ben drew and fired. The sounds of the shots were magnified in the saloon. Ben knew that he had killed Leo. He spun to try to get a shot at Trevor. Before he could do so he was amazed to see Trevor collapse in a pool of his own blood.

'I never did like to see two against one,' said Grizzly, holding his smoking revolver casually in his hand.

CHAPTER 10

Ben's feeling of relief was slightly marred when he discovered that he had blood on his left shoulder. At first the ridiculous thought occurred that somehow Leo's blood had spurted over him. Then realization of the truth dawned. He had been hit by Leo's shot.

'You'd better go up to your room,' said the barman, after handing Ben a towel to try to stop the blood. 'I'll send for the doc.'

Up in his room Ben was able to examine the wound in his shoulder. The hole was plain to see where the bullet had entered. Whether as the result of delayed shock, or for whatever reason, his shoulder was now aching abominably.

He managed to get his shirt off with every movement being a painful one. He used the shirt to try to stem the blood which was still oozing out of the wound.

So you weren't as clever as you thought, were you?
I killed Leo, didn't I?
Yes, and if his bullet had been a couple of inches to the right he would have killed you.
Maybe I'm getting too old for shoot-outs in a bar.
Maybe you should settle down with a nice wife and give up this dangerous life.
What do you mean – a nice wife? Have you got anybody in mind?
Well, there's Dora. She's attractive, intelligent—
You can forget about her. She'll be off to some godforsaken part of the country in a few days' time.

His thoughts were interrupted by the arrival of the maid. She was a jolly forty-year-old who always had a ready smile. However, at the sight of the blood on the shirt that Ben was holding against his wound her face fell.

'You are in a mess, aren't you.' she said.

The doctor, when he arrived ten minutes later, confirmed it.

'You've lost a lot of blood,' he stated.

'I know. Most of it's on my shirt.'

'I always like dealing with a person with a sense of humour. It makes my next statement easier to swallow.'

The pain that Ben was feeling in his shoulder was mirrored in the expression on his face.

'Don't say I'm going to lose the use of my arm.'

'No, you're lucky. The bullet went straight through. I'm bandaging it up now. You'll have to stay in bed for a few days to give the wound a chance to heal. The longer you stay in bed, the better the chance will be of it healing completely. Do you want anything to ease the pain?'

Ben was on the point of refusing, then he changed his mind.

'I suppose I might as well have something. After all, Pinkerton's will be paying. They don't pay us much when we're on duty, but when we're dying they can be quite generous.'

The doctor smiled.

'That's what I like to see,' said Ben. 'A doctor with a sense of humour.'

'*Touché*' came the reply.

The laudanum that the doctor gave him and the doses which the maid periodically administered meant that he slept heavily for the next couple of days. The doctor, when he came again, examined the wound.

'It looks pretty healthy to me,' he said. 'I'll put some fresh bandages on it.'

'Can I get up now?' demanded Ben.

'You can walk around the room if you like.'

'Is that all?'

'What else did you have in mind?'

'I don't know. I thought maybe I'd go down to

the dining-room and have a decent meal.'

'You can go when I say so. I'm cutting down on your doses of laudanum, but I still want you to take it.'

'I've read about people getting addicted to that stuff.'

'I know. That's why I'm cutting down on your dosage.'

'You've got an answer for everything, haven't you?'

'If I had I wouldn't be working in a town like this. I'd be in New York getting richer every day.'

'We all have our cross to bear, Doc,' said Ben, solicitously.

Some time later the maid knocked and entered.

'I'm not due for another dose of laudanum yet, am I?' demanded Ben.

'No. You've got a visitor. A lady visitor. I just wanted to see if you're ready to receive her.'

'A lady?'

'She's one of the religious company who are going on the wagon train.'

It was indeed Dora who entered. She was wearing a colourful blouse and black skirt. She came in rather diffidently.

'Sit down,' said Ben, patting the edge of the bed. 'I'm sorry the seating is rather limited.'

She smiled.

'That's the best tonic a sick man could have.'

'What is?'

'Just to see you smile.'

'I've been talking to the doctor. He says he's been giving you laudanum. I can see it's made you delirious.'

'You know that you've risked your reputation by coming to see me. Word will get around that you've visited a man who was in bed.'

'I often visit the sick and dying. One more visit will go unnoticed.'

'It's lovely to see you,' said Ben, changing from the bantering tone he had been using to a more heartfelt one.

'Perhaps you won't say that when you know the real reason for my visit.'

'Try me.'

'It's about the man who calls himself Grizzly Smalls.'

'What about him?' Ben shifted in the bed to try to make himself more comfortable. She spotted his effort.

'Sit up,' she commanded.

He did so. She leaned over and seized the pillow. Her hair brushed his cheek as she straightened the pillow. For a moment their heads were almost touching. Ben could smell the faint scent of lavender on her blouse. It took an enormous amount of will power not to take her in his arms – or at least in his good arm, and kiss her.

'What about Grizzly Smalls?' He repeated the question in an effort to get his racing thoughts back back on an even keel.

'He shot the other outlaw.'

'That's right. He killed Trevor Wakely. If he hadn't killed him, I wouldn't be here now.'

'I can understand you being grateful to him.'

'Eternally grateful.'

'He'll be entitled to bounty money.'

'That's right.' He couldn't see where this discussion was heading.

'If he receives that bounty money how much will he get?'

'I'm not exactly sure. It all depends on the importance of the outlaw.'

'You mean how many people he's killed?'

'More or less.'

'Have a guess how much Mr Smalls will receive for killing Wakely.'

'I'd say three hundred dollars. It could even be more.'

'Three hundred dollars.' She nodded as though it confirmed her own thoughts.

'I'd say it's worth it for saving my life.'

'You're missing the point.'

'Am I?'

'If Mr Smalls receives three hundred dollars

bounty money he won't want the two hundred dollars we're offering him for taking the wagons out West.'

'I see.' There was a pause while Ben digested the implication.

'You agree with my assessment of the situation?'

'Absolutely.'

'Is that all you can say?' She flared up.

'What else can I say? It means that you won't be going on the wagon train as you had planned.'

'My father had set his heart on that wagon train.'

Ben kept a diplomatic silence.

'It has been his whole life for the past few months. He has talked about nothing else. He's organized it and now it will all come to nothing.'

'I wouldn't say that. Maybe in a year's time, when Grizzly has spent all his bounty money in a saloon, you can start planning it again.'

'In a year's time the enthusiasm for going West will have gone. The people will have settled here. A few of them might even have died. No, if the wagon train is to go then it's now or never.'

'Then, as you say, it might be never.' Already the horizon was becoming brighter. If the wagon train didn't go ahead as planned it meant that Dora would be staying here. He could even envisage the possibility of himself giving up his dangerous way of life and settling in Carlton. After all, there were far worse towns in the West in which to settle.

'Of course, there is another possibility.'

He'd been so wrapped up in his thoughts that he didn't really grasp her statement. Eventually he responded.

'What possibility?'

'Would you say that Grizzly realizes he is entitled to the bounty money?'

'Probably not. As soon as I get up I'll go to see him.'

'The wagon train's going in three days' time. If you didn't get up, then you couldn't tell him, could you?'

'That's pretty obvious, isn't it?'

'What would it take for you not to leave your bed until after the wagon train has gone?'

What was she suggesting? Surely not what he was thinking. As she had been speaking she had seemed to lean closer to him. Or was it his imagination?

'It would be going against my principles.'

Yes, she was definitely leaning closer. She was even licking her lips provocatively.

'I'm willing to do anything for my father. Since my mother died he has been father and mother to me. That's something you'll never understand. If I'm willing to put on one side everything I've been brought up to believe in, then it surely shouldn't be too hard for you to put aside one of your principles.'

So saying she slipped off her blouse.

CHAPTER 11

'He's killed Leo?' Ossler's cry of disbelief could be heard hundreds of yards away. Lucky that they were in a secluded valley, thought Snowy, who had been the bearer of the bad tidings.

'And Grizzly Smalls killed Trevor.'

Ossler was pacing up and down like a caged lion. The remaining outlaws had never seen him in such a rage.

'Where are their bodies now?' demanded Filey.

'In the undertaker's.'

'Who's going to bury them?' persisted Filey.

'What difference does it make?' screamed Ossler. 'They're dead, aren't they?'

'We can't go to their funeral,' Hanson pointed out reasonably. 'Otherwise the sheriff will know we're in the same gang.'

'I would have thought that's obvious,' snapped Ossler.

'What are we going to do?' demanded Snowy. 'There are only four of us now.'

'It makes it all the more important that we join the wagon train and meet up with the Smith gang,' said Ossler, in a more normal tone of voice.

'They say the wagon train's moving off at the end of the week,' said Snowy.

'Did you order a wagon when you were in town?' demanded Ossler.

'Yes, there's a farmer named Tillotson. He's got a wagon for sale. I bought it for two hundred dollars.'

'Two hundred dollars? That's a lot for a wagon,' said Filey.

'It's not just for the wagon, you fool,' said Snowy. 'It's also for the four horses.'

'Who are you calling a fool?' snarled Filey.

'All right. We don't want any quarrelling,' stated Ossler. 'When are we going to pick up the wagon?'

'Tomorrow.'

'Right. We've got to make sure we've got enough provisions. At least to get us as far as Herford.'

'There's one thing we should take with us,' said Hanson.

'What's that?' demanded Snowy.

'Bibles.'

The three regarded him with a mixture of disbelief and amusement.

'Yes, Bibles,' repeated Hanson. 'These are all religious guys we're going with. They'll know their Bibles. We've got to convince them that we're religious guys too. So we should have Bibles.'

'You know, you're quite right,' said Ossler.

Hanson was pleased to have some praise from the boss.

'It's my turn to go into town. I'll get four Bibles while I'm there.'

'I used to read the Bible when I was younger,' said Filey.

'I didn't know you could read,' said Snowy.

'All right you two, I said that's enough,' shouted Ossler.

'We're all on edge, boss,' said Hanson. 'The twins being killed has put us all on edge.'

'Yeah, I suppose you're right,' said Ossler. 'We'll open a bottle of whiskey and have a farewell drink to them.'

Snowy passed him a bottle of whiskey from among the provisions he had brought back from town.

Ossler opened the bottle and took a large pull.

'To absent friends,' he said, before passing the bottle on. The other three echoed the sentiment.

'What do we know about this Nolan?' demanded Ossler, when the ceremony was finished.

'He works for Pinkerton's,' supplied Snowy. 'One of the guys in the saloon said that he was wounded when Leo shot at him.'

'Did he say how badly he was wounded?'

'No. Except that he was staying in the saloon and the doctor had been to see him.'

'What are you going to do about him, boss?' demanded Hanson. 'Are you going to let him get away with killing Leo?'

Ossler took a swig at the whiskey.

'No, we'll deal with him before we go on the wagon train.'

'We're all with you there,' said Snowy.

'We'll get him just before we hit the trail. That way we could be miles away before the sheriff finds him,' said Ossler.

'What about the other guy?' demanded Filey. 'Are we going to let him get away with killing Trevor?'

'I don't understand why this guy Smalls got involved in the gunfight,' said Ossler.

'From what I heard he said he didn't like to see two guys against one,' said Snowy.

'That's very public-spirited of him,' sneered Ossler.

'Is he the guy in charge of the wagon train?' demanded Filey.

'That's him,' said Snowy.

'Then it shouldn't be too difficult to send him to boot hill, should it?' persisted Filey.

'We'll wait until we reach Herford. Then we'll say goodbye to the wagon train and Smalls,' said Ossler, as he passed on the whiskey bottle.

CHAPTER 12

In the sheriff's office the sheriff was having a serious discussion with his deputy.

'That's three killings in a week in which Nolan has been involved,' he stated.

'You can't really blame him for any of them,' said Charlie. Everybody in the town knew him as Charlie – few knowing that his real name was Willoughby.

'No, I suppose not.' The sheriff sighed. 'He certainly helped us out when Blight was holding the children hostage. By the way, how is he now?'

'I went to see him this morning. He's out of bed. He still seems a bit groggy.'

'He had a bullet in his shoulder, didn't he?'

'That's right. The doctor says it went straight through. Apparently if it had been a couple of inches to the right it would have gone into his heart.'

'So he was lucky,' mused the sheriff.

'It seems like it.'

'Right. To come back to the important point – two outlaws have been killed. What are we going to do about it?'

'I asked Nolan whether he thought that they were members of the gang who stole the rifles. He said it was possible – although he couldn't be definitely sure.'

'So let's assume that they were members of the gang – you know what that means?'

'That the rest of the gang are somewhere nearby?'

'Exactly.'

'You know what that also means?'

'That we've got to go and look for them.'

'Charlie, you're on the ball today.' The sheriff moved in his chair which creaked in protest.

'So we'll have to get a posse together.'

'You will, Charlie – not we. I'm getting too old to ride with a posse.'

You mean you're too fat, thought Charlie, privately. Aloud he said: 'When do I start?'

'Let's see. The earliest we could get a posse together would be Saturday.'

'The snag with getting a posse together is that we've got to let everybody in town know. That means if the outlaws are still around then they'll also know what we're doing.'

'That's one way of looking at it. Of course

there is another way.'

'What's that?'

'If the outlaws know that we're getting a posse together they might decide to move on. In which case it solve all our troubles.'

'But then we won't catch them,' protested Charlie.

'Exactly. We'll have got rid of them and without a shot being fired.'

'I thought we were supposed to uphold the law,' said Charlie, stubbornly.

'When will you learn, Charlie? We are here to survive. That's our first aim. I've been here now for twenty years. In that time all the sheriffs in the towns around have been killed. Most of them by outlaws. Survival is the name of the game in this job, Charlie. If we can drive the outlaws away from the town by advertising the fact that we're going to raise a posse in a couple of day's time, then it will be the ideal solution all round.'

At that moment there was a knock at the door and Sam entered. The sheriff waved him to a chair.

'What can we do for you, Sam?' he asked.

'You told me to keep you informed about when we will be leaving.'

'That's right, although whenever it is we'll be sorry to see you go.'

'Everything is arranged for Saturday. The wagon train will be starting early in the morning.'

'It's all happening on Saturday,' said Charlie. When he saw the puzzled expression on Sam's face he explained about the posse.

'Well, I hope you catch the outlaws,' said Sam.

'Have you got all the provisions you need?' asked the sheriff.

'Yes, I think we've got enough food. Anyhow if we haven't got enough we'll be stopping at Herford on the way. We can stock up with any last-minute provisions there.'

'I know you're a religious group, Sam, and as such you don't like killing anything, but have you made sure that you have enough guns?' demanded the sheriff. 'You'll want them to kill rabbits, deer or wild pigs to help your food supply.'

'Yes, we've got a few guns. As you say they could come in useful. One other thing I've got on my list which I must get in town today is dynamite.'

'What do you want dynamite for? You're not going to blow anything up, are you?' demanded Charlie.

'No. Mr Smalls said we might need it. Where we're going there could be fallen rocks or even landslides. The dynamite could come in useful.'

Sam took his leave shortly afterwards, with a promise that he would call in before the wagon train finally left.

CHAPTER 13

Ben was in the bar of the Red Garter saloon having the first drink he had had since the gunfight. The bartender spotted Ben's obvious enjoyment.

'I can see you enjoyed that,' he observed.

'After a week's abstinence it certainly tastes nice,' said Ben. 'So nice in fact that I think I'll have another.' He drained his glass.

'This one's on the house,' said the barman.

'Thanks, but there's no need . . .'

'Oh, I've gained out of the gunfight,' said the barman. 'This one's in the way of being a thank you.'

'How did you gain out of it?' asked Ben, accepting the drink.

'People have been coming here just to see the place where the gunfight took place. Of course they've been ordering drinks while they've been here.'

'Of course,' said Ben, drily.

'I was going to take the bullets out of the wall, but the visitors like to see them, so I've left them there.'

Ben smiled. 'I'm glad that me almost getting killed has been of benefit to you.'

'There's even some of your blood by the door which I point out to the visitors.'

Ben chuckled. 'Maybe I could donate my shirt with the blood on it.'

'Ah, well . . .' The bartender's guilty expression told Ben that he had hit the nail on the head.

'Don't tell me. You haven't thrown it away as I thought. You've kept it.'

'Well, yes. But I haven't used it as an exhibit. Not until I've had your permission.'

Ben was about to refuse. However, on second thoughts he changed his mind. The bartender and the maid had both been kind when he had been recovering from the wound – particularly the maid.

'That's OK. You can use it as an exhibit.'

The bartender smiled. 'Thanks. Have another drink on the house.'

'I'll have a whiskey. Oh, and I'd like to leave a donation for the maid. She did a good job looking after me when I was in bed.' Ben took a few dollar bills from his wallet and placed them on the bar.

When the barman returned he placed them behind the bar in an empty tankard.

'Between you and me,' he said, 'I'm thinking of asking Milly to marry me.'

'I hope your proposal will be accepted,' said Ben. 'Then if you ever get shot you'll have somebody who, I recommend, will take care of you.'

'Her husband died about a year back. I've waited until now before I propose.'

'My advice is don't wait any longer,' said Ben. 'You never know what's round the corner.'

'You're right. I'll ask her this evening,' said the bartender. 'Let me buy you another drink,' he said, seeing that Ben had emptied his whiskey-glass.

Ben glanced round the bar. There was the usual card-school in the usual corner. When the bartender had refilled his glass Ben asked: 'Have you seen much of Grizzly Smalls? I want to buy him a drink for saving my life – a few drinks in fact.'

'Oh, he's done well out of saving your life.'

'How do you mean?'

'He was always a good story-teller. Now he's got a story which caps all the others. So he's going round the saloons in the town telling the listeners how he saved the life of a Pinkerton agent. Of course he's put a stretch on the tale. According to his version his gun was in his holster when the two brothers went for their guns. It was his speed in drawing his gun that saved your life.'

'I was too busy shooting Leo to notice where Grizzly's gun was,' confessed Ben.

'I've heard his version,' said the bartender. 'In it you are almost dying from your bullet wound. When he walks in here and sees you he'll have to alter his story.'

'Tell him I made a quick recovery,' said Ben.

At that moment a young lad came into the saloon.

'No children allowed in here,' said the bartender, automatically.

The boy ignored him and approached Ben.

'Are you the man whose life was saved by Grizzly Smalls?'

'You could say that.'

'There's a lady outside who says she wants to see you.'

'I'll be out in two minutes,' said Ben, as he hastily finished his drink.

'I wouldn't hurry if I were you,' said the lad. 'She's spitting mad.'

CHAPTER 14

In the church hall three men – the preacher, Harry and Paul – were attending a meeting which had been hastily called by the preacher. It was obvious from the preacher's face that he had some important news to share with them.

'Don't say there are some last-minute hitches,' said Harry.

'I'm afraid so,' said Sam. 'In fact the biggest last-minute hitch that there could be. We're not going tomorrow.'

The fact that both men were stunned by the news was reflected on their faces. 'Why on earth not?' demanded Paul.

Sam's answer was to place a bundle of dollar notes on the table.

'What are those?' demanded Harry.

'It's the two hundred dollars we gave to Mr Smalls to take the wagon train,' replied Sam, bitterly.

'Now he's not going to take us,' stated Paul.

'Exactly.'

'Why not? Isn't it enough?' demanded Harry.

'Oh, it's nothing to do with the money. Although I suppose it is in a way. He's come into some money from another source.'

'Whatever the source he can't be getting as much as two hundred dollars,' stated Harry.

'Apparently he can. In fact he's going to get three hundred dollars.'

'You mean he's come into a legacy?' demanded Paul.

Sam permitted himself a grim smile. 'You could say he's inherited money from somebody's death.'

Suddenly comprehension appeared on Paul's face. 'He killed that outlaw in a saloon, didn't he?'

'That's right.'

'Now he's going to receive bounty money for it.'

'Right again. Three hundred dollars.'

'So what do we do?' demanded Harry.

'What can we do?' replied Sam, with all the bitterness of a person who had seen his long-treasured hopes dashed at one blow.

Ben found Dora seated in the café. In fact, because of the earliness of the hour, she was the only person there, although shortly, when some of the town's women had finished their shopping they would be calling in.

Her greeting was far from friendly. In fact the waitress behind the counter discreetly disappeared into the back room when she heard Dora's first words.

'You bastard!'

'I didn't know that you swore,' said Ben, mildly.

'Believe me, where my family came from that's a mild oath.'

'You've got something on your mind?'

'Of course I have, you bastard.'

'Am I to deduce that I should know what it is?'

'Of course you do, you—'

'Hold it. Let's leave my ancestry out of this, shall we?'

The vitriol slowly disappeared from her tones. 'You promised me.'

Realization dawned on Ben.

'This is about Grizzly Smalls, isn't it'?'

'You promised me you wouldn't tell him that he was due to get bounty money for killing the outlaw.'

'I kept my promise. I haven't seen Grizzly Smalls since the time he shot Trevor Wakely.'

Her eyes searched his face as she tried to assess whether he was lying.

'You swear it?' she said, eventually.

'Yes. On the Bible.'

She took a deep breath. 'I've made a fool of myself, haven't I?'

'You jumped to a conclusion, that's all. It was a natural mistake to make.'

She clenched and unclenched her hands several times.

'If you didn't tell him, who did?'

'He probably worked it out himself. He's been around a lot. He may even have had bounty money for killing somebody else in the past.'

'I suppose you could be right.'

The waitress reappeared and Ben ordered coffees.

'What do we do now?' asked Dora, half to herself.

'It all depends whether you still want to go.'

'Of course we do. But if Smalls isn't prepared to take us, what chance have we got?'

The coffees arrived. Dora stared out through the window. Her face was a picture of dejection.

'Of course there is an alternative,' said Ben, eventually.

She turned towards him. 'Which is?'

Ben dipped his finger in his almost empty coffee-cup. He made a cross on the table.

'Carlton.' He made another cross some distance away. 'Herford.' His next move was to make a circle about a couple of feet away from the cross. 'Indian territory.'

She watched with interest.

'Where does that get us?'

'It shows that you are starting from the wrong place. If you want a guide to take you to the Indian territories you are far more likely to find one in Herford than in Carlton. You were lucky to find Smalls here.'

She leaned forward. There was a gleam of excitement in her eyes.

'So what you're saying is that we should go ahead with the wagon train. We can get to Herford ourselves. After all, the stage goes there once a week. Then when we get there we look around for a train manager.'

'Exactly.'

She stared at him while she absorbed the full force of his suggestion. At last a smile lit up her face.

'You know, I could kiss you.'

'You said you would come to bed with me, but nothing came of it.'

'You really are a bastard, aren't you,' she said, as she stood up. The smile on her face took the sting out of her words.

CHAPTER 15

Although the wagons were due to set off as soon as possible after dawn a large crowd had already gathered to see them off. Sam himself had taken charge of seeing that the wagons were properly secured and that the harnesses of the horses were tight. He went along the row of wagons accompanied by Harry and Paul.

'I hope you're right in assuming that we will be able to find a wagon master in Herford,' said Harry.

'Well, we should stand a very good chance,' said Sam. 'After all, it's the nearest town to the Indian territory. There must be several people there who can take us to our new home.'

'Anyhow we've still got the money to pay somebody,' said Paul.

Dora joined her father as he moved along the wagons.

'I hope your friend is right about there being a wagon master in Herford,' he whispered to her.

'I hope so too. And he's not my friend.'

'I must be mistaken. I thought, since you went to visit him after he had been shot, that you were on friendly terms.'

'Ben Nolan means nothing to me,' she asserted.

'Then why do you keep looking around as if you expected to see him?'

'He was the one who advised us to go to Herford and pick up a wagon master there.'

'Let's hope he's right,' said her father as he proceeded to check the wagons. He came to the last wagon. Ossler was standing by the horses.

'Is everything ready?' demanded the preacher, casting a critical eye over the closed wagon.

'Yes, we're all ready to go.'

'I thought there were more of you.'

'The others are in the wagon.'

'I see. What about food? We've got plenty of provisions at least to get us to Herford.'

'You don't have to worry about us. We've brought our own provisions.'

'That seems to be it then,' said Sam, returning to where his daughter was standing.

'I suppose so,' she said, listlessly.

'You don't seem very excited at the prospect of going.'

'I suppose it's the thought of leaving all this behind.' She waved an arm to indicate the people and town.

'You'll soon change your mind once we're on the road.'

At that moment Ben rode in. Some of the bystanders moved to one side as he jumped down from his horse. He went up to Dora and gave her a bunch of flowers.

'Beautiful flowers for a beautiful lady.'

'I seem to have heard that line before,' she said, with a smile.

'You're supposed to say: I'll miss you,' he said.

'I *will* miss you. I'll miss my friends. I'll miss this ugly town . . .' She was getting quite emotional.

'You'll change your mind once you get on the road.'

'You sound just like my father,' she said, crossly.

There were signs of restless movements from the horses. Most of the wagon-owners had jumped up on the buckboards. In the last wagon a heated argument was taking place.

'We can still kill him,' said Hanson. The three inside the wagon were studying Ben's movements through a gap in the canvas.

'How do you propose to do it,' said Filey. 'Just shoot him now?'

'We should have killed him yesterday,' said Snowy.

'The boss decided that it was too risky,' said Filey. 'With the sheriff getting a posse together the best thing we could do was to keep our heads down until we had the chance to get out of the town.'

'Who's that girl he's talking to?' demanded Hanson.

'That's the preacher's daughter. She's coming on the wagon train with us,' said Snowy.

'She's lovely. I wouldn't mind taking up religion myself if there are more like her around.'

It was obvious that they had agreed there was no way they could proceed with their stated intention of killing Ben. They settled down as comfortably as they could in between the rifles.

Whistles were being blown to show that everybody was ready.

'This is it,' said Dora, holding out her hand.

'You remember in the coffee-house that you said you could kiss me?'

'Ye-es.'

'Well I've come for my payment.'

He took her in his arms. For a brief moment she struggled. Then her resistance changed and she clung to him in a long passionate embrace.

'I thought she said he didn't mean anything to her,' observed her father drily.

CHAPTER 16

Ben watched the last wagon disappearing out of sight with mixed feelings. It would have been great if Dora had stayed in Carlton. She was the sort of woman he would have liked to have spent time with and got to know better. But she'd gone out of his life for ever and he'd better accept it.

The doctor had said that he should take some exercise to build up his strength. His response was to ride as fast as he could – although in the opposite direction to the one the wagons had taken. He wasn't sure whether the doctor would include riding among the best forms of exercise, but this morning that was what he felt like doing.

He loved the exhilarating feeling of riding a horse at a gallop. He loved the clean wind on his face driving away any conflict in his mind. He often found that galloping was the best means of settling any problems he might have.

Not that he had any problems at the moment. It would have been nice, though, if Dora had stayed in Carlton. Why did the picture of her starting to strip by his bedside keep coming to his mind? He spurred his horse viciously.

Later that morning he called in at the sheriff's office. Both the sheriff and the deputy were there. The sheriff indicated a chair.

'I don't suppose the posse found anything,' said Ben, as he sat down.

'You're right,' said Charlie. 'We did find a camp a few miles outside the town. It looked as though it had been used by a few men for several days. They had left their empty tins of food and whiskey bottles lying around.'

'Any idea when they left?'

'Fairly recently, I'd say. The ashes from their fire were cold, but the wind hadn't scattered them yet. So maybe the rest of the gang took flight when two of them were killed.'

'If the camp belonged to the gang that you are after and if they did take flight when two of them were killed, they'll be far away by now,' suggested the sheriff.

Charlie made some coffees.

'It was a sad occasion this morning to see the wagon train leaving,' suggested the sheriff.

'Yeah, they were keen on going,' stated Ben.

'I hope they're not going out of the frying-pan

into the fire,' said Charlie.

'What do you mean?'

'We've had several reports recently about a couple of the Indian tribes stirring up trouble in their territories.'

'So things are not as settled in their part of the world as they are supposed to be?' asked Ben.

'That's the impression we've got during these past few weeks,' said the sheriff.

'Did you tell the preacher and his followers this?'

'I tried to. But he wouldn't listen. Sam could be very strong-minded at times.'

'Just like his daughter,' said Ben, half to himself.

He finished his coffee and left shortly afterwards, promising before he went that he would let them know when he intended to return to Chicago.

That evening, when he was in the bar of the Setting Sun, he saw a familiar figure enter.

'Grizzly,' he said. 'I hear you've been doing a royal tour of the saloons in Carlton.'

'All twenty-two of them,' said Grizzly proudly. 'I had to make sure they all knew the truth about our shoot-out here with the outlaws.'

'The truth which has been embellished a bit,' suggested Ben.

'All good stories have to be decorated a bit,'

replied Grizzly. 'By the way, how are you after your bit of trouble?'

'I'm pretty well recovered thanks. Let me buy you a drink for saving my life.'

When they were seated in a corner, Grizzly said: 'Here's to successful gunfights.'

Ben downed his drink.

'As long as they don't come around too often,' he replied.

'You heard that I'm a rich man now,' Grizzly informed him.

'Yes, I heard the good news. That you were paid the bounty money for killing one of the twins.'

'I had bounty money once before. A long time ago,' Grizzly confided. 'But then it was only fifty dollars. This time it was three hundred.'

'So there was no need for you to take the preacher and his followers to the Indian territory?'

'That's right. Anyhow now isn't a good time to take them. The Indians are getting angry.'

'What about?'

'They've been swindled out of some of their land. At least the Sioux Indians have. Some government agents have been double-crossing them. They've been getting their leaders to sign away more of their land than they thought they were giving up.'

'Is that bad news for the preacher and his followers?'

'It could be. Especially since the Sioux have started doing the ghost dance.'

'The ghost dance? What's that?'

'They paint their skin red. They wear a special white robe. They dance in a circle for hours and hours. At the end of it some even die of exhaustion. They think the dance purifies them for their struggle against the white man.'

'And you say there are more of these ghost dances going on now?'

'That's what I've heard on the grapevine.'

A worried Ben ordered another round of drinks.

'Of course when the preacher and his followers get to Herford they'll hear all about this,' he stated.

'The question is will they put aside their plan to go to the Indian territories,' said Grizzly.

CHAPTER 17

The following morning, Sunday, Ben went for a ride. Charlie had told him where the posse had found the camp which might have been used by the outlaws. He arrived there and dismounted. While his horse was grazing he studied the remains of the camp.

There was ample evidence of a few horsemen who had stayed there. Judging by the number of empty whiskey bottles they must have stayed there for several days. It could fit in with them being the gang who had stolen the rifles from the train – but there was nothing concrete to justify the assumption.

Whoever had camped there had built a large fire to get rid of any possible evidence of their residence there. That in itself might be suspicious or might not. How many men had stayed here? And were they the outlaws he was searching for? He kicked one of the empty whiskey-bottles in frustration.

Later in the morning he was walking in the town, having left his horse in the livery stable. He was walking along Main Street when he suddenly heard the sound of singing. A couple of hundred yards further on he identified the source. It was a church. On impulse he pushed open the door and slipped inside.

The congregation were singing, 'Nearer my God to Thee'. For a fleeting moment he had a vivid picture of another group of religious enthusiasts being massacred by Indians. He quickly thrust the thought aside.

What was he doing here anyhow? He rarely went to church. Well, only to funerals and weddings. So why had his footsteps led him into this building, seemingly by their own volition? It must be because he felt guilty about sending Dora and the other Christians into danger. Both Charlie and Grizzly had stressed that there could be danger in going into the Indian Territories at present. Which was exactly what Dora and the others intended to do.

What could he do about it? Nothing. He was here in Carlton. He would send a telegram to Pinkerton headquarters in Chicago, informing them that the gang of outlaws had probably moved on. Then he would await further instructions. He had already sent a letter to them giving a description of the incident in which he had been wounded. It had been a routine letter. The rate of wounding and even killings among Pinkerton employees was quite high and the director wouldn't be particularly surprised by his report.

The preacher had now indicated that the congregation would sing the next hymn. It was 'Abide with me, fast falls the eventide.' When the singing started Ben slipped unnoticed out of the church.

That evening after dinner he had had more to drink than he usually did. In deference to the fact that it was Sunday the usual saloon singer wasn't in evidence. Ben found himself watching a game of cards.

'Why don't you join in, Mr Nolan?' asked one of the players.

'I don't want him to join in,' said one of the others. 'If he's as quick in dealing cards as he is with a gun, he'll be dealing them from the bottom of the pack.'

There was general laughter.

'The way my luck is going these days I would probably lose all my money in the first ten minutes,' replied Ben.

'You're the ideal person we're looking for,' said the first player to more laughter.

'We've had a couple of guys joining us these last few days,' said another, 'But they must have moved on. In fact one of them seemed interested in you after you were shot. He kept asking one question after another. In the end we had to tell him to shut up and get on with playing cards.'

'They could be two of the outlaws I'm looking for,' said Ben. 'Could you describe them?'

The efforts of the four card-players to provide descriptions didn't help Ben to get a clear picture of them.

'I don't suppose you got their names,' demanded Ben.

'Oh, yes,' replied one of the players. 'The one was called Hanson and the other was called Filey.'

Hanson and Filey. Ben repeated the names to himself as he took up his usual position by the bar. Were they two of the names on the outlaws' wall in Pinkerton's? Well, he would have to wait until the tomorrow before he could send a telegram there to find out.

CHAPTER 18

The following morning Ben presented himself at the telegraph office as soon as it was being opened.

'You're early,' observed the telegraph officer.

'I've got an important telegram to send,' Ben informed him.

He sent the telegram to headquarters asking them to check to see whether Hanson and Filey were wanted outlaws.

'You might get a reply this afternoon,' said the officer. 'If not you should get it tomorrow morning.'

'Thanks,' said Ben.

He called in at the coffee-house. It, too, was just opened.

'Your friend has gone,' observed the waitress, as she served his coffee.

'Friend? Oh, yes.' He remembered the last

94

time he had been there with Dora. Was it only three days ago? It seemed like an eternity.

The wagon train would be well on its way to Herford by now. It had been on the trail for two days and unless there was a hitch it should have put quite a few miles behind it. The trail was a good one to Herford – the stage used it regularly and unless there was any hold-up due to the weather – such as heavy rain flooding part of the trail, then the wagons should make good time. Since there hadn't been any heavy rain recently there was nothing to prevent the wagons doing at least, say, fifteen miles a day. They might even do as much as eighteen miles if they started early and kept going until dusk. Why did he keep thinking about the wagon train, he wondered gloomily as he finished his coffee.

He called in at the sheriff's office. The sheriff hadn't yet arrived, but Charlie was there.

'Have you got two outlaws named Hanson and Filey on your wanted list?' asked Ben.

'I don't think so,' replied Charlie. 'Their names don't strike a chord. But I'll make sure.'

He scanned the drawings on the notice board.

'No, they're not there,' he announced. Then he drew out a pile of drawings from the desk drawer. He flipped through them slowly while Ben watched impatiently. When he came to the last one he said: 'No. There are no outlaws named Hanson and Filey here either. What is your interest in them?'

Ben explained that they had been two card-players in the Setting Sun who had vanished on the night before the wagon train had started. And that they had been particularly interested in his own whereabouts.

'They could be two of the gang,' Charlie conceded. 'On the other hand it might be a coincidence'

The sheriff arrived and his deputy put him in the picture.

'You could be right,' he informed Ben. 'When we advertised the fact that we were going to raise the posse it's likely the gang became scared and rode off.'

'The question is, if they were the outlaws we are looking for how did they move the guns and ammunition?' asked Ben.

'Maybe they bought a covered wagon,' suggested the sheriff.

'Yes, that's a possibility,' admitted Ben.

The sheriff came to a decision. 'Charlie, you go to the farms around the town. Find out whether any of them sold a wagon to some strangers in the last few days.'

'Probably three or four days ago,' suggested Ben. He stood up.

'What are you going to do?' demanded the sheriff.

'I'm going back to where you found that camp where the outlaws might have stayed. I didn't think of it at the time, but there could be some signs that they had a wagon there.'

Ben rode out to the camp, pleased that he had something definite to do. Just hanging around the town waiting for the reply to his telegram would be irksome. Especially since he probably wouldn't receive a reply until the following morning.

The campsite was as deserted as on his previous visit, except for the crows who protested noisily at the intruder interrupting their meal. Ben dismounted and began searching the ground for any signs of wagon wheels.

He found them about a hundred yards away from the camp on a piece of flat land. Yes, there were definite wheel-marks. Ben stared at them thoughtfully. They proved beyond reasonable doubt that the outlaws who had camped here were the ones he was looking for, since it would be too much of a coincidence to have another group of travellers who owned a wagon and who were camping a short distance from the town. He tried to follow the direction the wagon had taken when it was driven from the site. However the ground around the camp was too hard. It would take a skilled tracker to be able to follow the direction the wagon had taken when it had left the camp.

Ben rode back to the town. He knew now that the outlaws had a wagon. When he arrived back at the sheriff's office he informed the sheriff of his find. He had just finished putting the sheriff in the picture when Charlie arrived, obviously bursting to impart his own information.

'I've found him,' he exclaimed.

'Who is he?' demanded the sheriff.

'It's a farmer named Tillotson.'

'He sold a wagon to the outlaws?'

'Yes. On Thursday last week.'

'It fits in,' said the sheriff. 'The twins were dead – you'd killed one and Grizzly the other. They knew the hunt for them would be warming up. So they bought the wagon and upped sticks and left.' There was a certain amount of relief in his voice that the outlaws were no longer in his territory.

'The farmer thought there was something suspicious about the two guys who bought it,' continued Charlie.

'In what way?' demanded Ben.

'Well the two guys who bought the wagon and horses didn't haggle. Tillotson named his price and they accepted it right away. Normally you don't do things that way. If you're buying something that costs a lot of money like that – you haggle.'

'Did this farmer say how much he charged them?'

'Two hundred dollars. He said the wagon had been sitting out in the back of the farm for months and the horses were shortly due for the knacker's yard. So he thinks he had a good deal.'

'It does sound like it, doesn't it?' said the sheriff, thoughtfully.

Ben told Charlie about him fording a camping-site that almost definitely belonged to the outlaws. 'The only thing we don't know, is which direction they took when they left the camp,' Ben concluded.

'And we don't know their identities,' added the sheriff.

'Two of them could be Hanson and Filey,' stated Ben. 'I'll call at the telegraph office this afternoon to see whether there's a telegram for me confirming this.'

During the afternoon the doctor called at the saloon to see Ben.

'I've come to see whether I can take that bandage off your wound,' he explained.

When the bandage came off he examined it critically.

'There's no pus,' he stated.

'Is that a good thing?' demanded Ben.

99

'It means the wound is clean. It should heal on its own from now on. I'm not going to put another bandage on it'

When the doctor was putting away his instruments he added: 'Are you taking exercise as I advised?'

'I'm doing quite a bit of riding.'

'Yes, that's not too bad I suppose. The best exercise is walking. There is one form of exercise I definitely wouldn't recommend though.'

'What's that, doc?'

'Gunfighting,' said the doctor, with a chuckle, as he went out through the door.

CHAPTER 19

There was no message in the telegraph office for Ben.

'Maybe it will be here the first thing in the morning,' said the officer.

'Yes, maybe,' replied Ben.

That evening, after he had had his dinner, he went into the bar. Grizzly was seated in a corner.

'I thought you'd still be telling them about how you saved my life,' said Ben, drily.

'They've all heard it by now. Still, I've got plenty of money to buy my own drinks now. Can I buy you one?'

'Why not?' said Ben.

When Grizzly returned he gave Ben his drink. Then he handed him a crumpled newspaper which had been concealed in his pocket.

'Read that,' he said, pointing to the headline. It said: INDIANS ON THE WARPATH. It described how the Lakota Sioux Indians were close to rebellion after a series of land deals with what they claimed were cheating land-registration officers. As a result the Indians had been forced to move out of their territories. The article described the ghost dance which several white men had witnessed recently. *It is only a matter of time,* concluded the article, *before the Indians take up arms and seek their revenge for the loss of their territories.*

There was a worried frown on Ben's face as he re-read the article which came from the Herford *Times.*

'I had it from my friend. He lives in Herford,' explained Grizzly.

'Dora and the Christians are going to the Indian territories,' stated Ben.

'So you've told me. If I were them I'd think twice about it.'

They were going to the Indian territories because he had pointed out to Dora how they could get there. If he had kept quiet it was possible that the Christians would have given up the idea of leaving Carlton. There had been no need for him to interfere. But no, you had to show her how clever you were. If you hadn't pointed out that they would find a guide in Herford, Dora would have stayed here. He would have enjoyed her company.

'Maybe they'll read this newspaper when they get to Herford,' said Grizzly, sensing his unease.

Ben didn't reply.

'How are you getting on with finding the rest of your outlaws?' Grizzly asked, later. 'Not that I want to shoot any of them.'

Ben gave a begrudging smile. He explained how they had probably discovered where the outlaws had camped. 'The problem is that we don't know in which direction the outlaws went.'

'You say they might have gone on Friday,' said Grizzly, keenly.

'That's right.'

'It hasn't rained since then, has it?'

'No. What's that got to do with it?'

'There could be enough evidence to find out which direction they went. If you know where to look for it.'

'Well I looked around a bit, but I couldn't find anything,' said Ben, irritably.

'Yes, but you were never an army scout were you?' said Grizzly, with more than a hint of satisfaction in his voice.

'You were, I suppose?'

'Private Glen Smalls, No. 7638 reporting,' replied Grizzly, giving a salute.

Ben regarded him thoughtfully. 'And as an army scout you think you can find evidence as to which direction the wagon took?'

'I learned to track under one of the best track-ers in the business – a Crow Indian.'

'Right, Private Smalls. I want you to report for duty outside this saloon at eight o'clock sharp tomorrow morning. Your task will be to find out which direction the wagon and the outlaws took after leaving the outlaws' camp.'

'Can't I report at nine o'clock?' demanded Grizzly.

'Eight o'clock. Or you'll be put on guard duty.'

'I did that often enough,' Grizzly confessed.

To Ben's surprise Grizzly was outside the saloon at the agreed time.

'I never get up at this time in the morning,' Grizzly grumbled, as they started off.

'It's good for the soul,' replied Ben.

When they arrived at the camp Grizzly dismounted. He began to wander around, peer-ing closely at the ground. His wandering took him some distance away from the camp. Ben, who had also dismounted, smoked one impa-tient cigarette after another while he waited.

After what seemed like an eternity Grizzly returned to where Ben was standing.

'The wagon came in one way and went out the other,' he announced.

'How do you know?'

'The wheel marks aren't so deep where the wagon came in. Also there was only one horse accompanying it.'

'There was a driver and one rider. That fits in with what the farmer who sold the wagon stated.'

'Then when the wagon left it was carrying a heavier load – you can see where the ruts are deeper.'

'I'll take your word for it.'

'This time there were three riders.'

'That would be it,' said Ben, excitedly. 'There are only four outlaws left. You and me having killed one each. Which direction did they take?'

'Towards Carlton.'

'What?' Surprise stretched Ben's voice. 'Why would they go towards Carlton? If they wanted to get away with the guns they should have gone in the opposite direction.'

'I wouldn't know. You're the detective.'

'You're positive about this?'

'I swear it on my mother's grave. I'd swear it on my father's too, but I never knew who he was.'

They rode slowly back to Carlton. The thought kept hammering at Ben's mind. Why would the outlaws go to Carlton when it would be safer for them to make their escape in the opposite direction?

The answer came like a blinding flash.

'Oh, no!' He groaned aloud.

The outlaws had taken their wagon to Carlton and tagged on to the wagon train. Unknowingly, the Christians had been accompanied by a gang of outlaws.

CHAPTER 20

The wagon train had been on the trail for three days, so far without any major hold-ups. There had been one incident a few hours back when a horse had shed its shoe. However they were fortunate that they had a blacksmith in one of the wagons and he was able to fix the horse with a new shoe while they had stopped for the morning break.

The mood among those on the wagon train was one of optimism. They were all anticipating starting a fresh life, away from the evils and temptations to be found in towns such as Carlton. They would establish an independent, God-fearing community. They had not only a blacksmith among their numbers, but also a young man who had spent a year training as a doctor. They also had a baker, butcher, and other tradesmen who would all contribute to their community. Some of them spoke the native Gaelic which had been handed down for centuries in the old country and one of their aims was to preserve the language.

Dora, too, was looking ahead to their arrival in the Indian territories with eagerness. On the trail she had lots of time to think. True, from time to time she found a mental picture of a certain Ben Nolan interrupting her thoughts. She remembered their last kiss with warm satisfaction. If she had stayed in Carlton there was no doubt that Ben was the sort of person she would have liked to see more of – but she had better get used to the idea that she would never see him again.

Her father, too, was in a more contented frame of mind than she had seen him for some considerable time.

'We're making good time,' he stated. 'If we keep going at this rate we could be in Herford in five days' time.'

'Yes, the weather has been kind to us,' she admitted.

'There's one thing I wish . . .'

'What's that?'

'That the men in the last wagon would join in the little service we hold at the end of each day. It's strange that they don't mix with us.'

'Yes, they do keep themselves to themselves,'

said Dora, reflectively.

'The man who seems to be their leader, Ossler, informed me that they were religious folk like us. That's why they were coming to the Indian territories. So you would think they would join in our little services.'

'They don't even join us when we're having our meal,' stated Dora. 'They say that they've brought their own food with them.'

'They say there are four of them, but I've only seen Ossler and one of the others.'

'His name is Hanson. He introduced himself to me. He considers himself to be a ladies' man.' There was more than a hint of scorn in her statement.

'So he's not in the same class as Mr Nolan,' observed her father, wryly.

'To put it bluntly,' she said, 'Hanson is scum.'

'He hasn't tried anything, has he?' demanded her father, with alarm.

'Of course not. I can look after myself.'

'If there are any problems, you'll let me know, won't you?'

'I promise I will,' she said, kissing him on the cheek.

Ben was in fact at that moment riding like the wind as he followed their trail. Having come to the conclusion that the outlaws were in one of the wagons on the wagon train he had wasted no time in setting off in pursuit. He had galloped back to the Setting Sun, leaving Grizzly in his wake. In fact, when Grizzly did arrive in the saloon he found that Ben had slung his few possessions into his saddle-bag and was ready to leave.

'They've got at least a couple of days' start on you,' said Grizzly. 'You'll be lucky to catch them before they reach Herford.'

'I know, but I've got to try.'

'Good luck,' said Grizzly, as he watched Ben ride away.

I'll need it, said Ben to himself as he galloped down Main Street.

CHAPTER 21

Sam's hope that they would reach Herford without further mishap was shattered when one of the wheels on a wagon snapped. The wagon was an old one that had seen considerable service on a farm.

'That family should never have brought that wagon,' said Paul. 'It's obvious that it's falling apart.'

'We must be charitable,' said Sam. 'They wanted so much to come with us.'

'The question is what are we going to do?' said Harry. 'We can't share them out between the rest of the wagons – they've got five children.'

The family in question were named the Turvilles.

'We can't have any of their children in our wagon,' said Paul. 'Not to put too fine a point on it, they're a disruptive influence.'

The blacksmith was examining the wheel.

'I can probably fix the wheel. It should hold until we get to Herford. After that they won't be able to take the wagon over the rough ground to the Indian territories.'

'How long will it take you to fix it?' demanded Sam.

'I don't know. Maybe a couple of hours.'

'I'll pass the message on,' said Paul. 'That we've got a wait of a couple of hours.'

The news was received with resignation by most of the travellers. Ossler, however, did not take kindly to the delay.

'We want to get to Herford as quickly as possible,' he snapped.

'It will only be a couple of hours,' said Paul, placatingly.

After Paul had left Ossler went inside the wagon to share the news with the three outlaws.

'Do we have to wait here?' demanded Snowy. 'We've got out of Carlton. There's nothing stopping us from leaving this lot and going ahead to Herford.'

'It's too risky,' said Ossler. 'We don't want to take any chances. Anyhow it's only a couple of hours. It will soon pass. You can get out the cards.'

'You can leave me out of the game,' said Hanson.

'Have you got bored with cards?' asked Ossler.

'Leave him alone,' said Filey. 'He's got a telescope.'

'What does he want a telescope for?' demanded Ossler.

'He's watching that attractive young lady in the leading wagon.'

'She's stretched out on the tail-board of their wagon,' stated Hanson. 'I wouldn't mind stretching out by her side.'

The delay of a couple of hours which the blacksmith had forecast proved to be wildly inaccurate. The hours dragged by and the wheel was showing no sign of being restored to its former shape.

The day was hot and Dora had left her place on the wagon and was sheltering under a tree. She was sleeping when she felt something tickling her behind her ear. Still half-asleep she brushed it aside. However the sensation didn't go away. The next time her gesture was an impatient one as she flicked at the annoying object. When it still didn't go away she opened her eyes to find out what had interrupted her sleep. When she realized its cause she jumped up. Hanson was standing there with a blade of grass in his hand, with which he had obviously been tickling her.

'What do you think you are doing?' she demanded.

'I'm sorry. It was just a bit of fun.'

'Well I don't think it's funny.' She started to move away.

'Don't go. I've got something to tell you. It's for your own benefit.'

She stopped a few yards away from him.

'I don't think I'd be interested in anything you have to tell me.'

'Why should a pretty young lady like you be tagging along with this lot?' He waved a hand indicating the wagons that were lined up along the trail.

'Because I choose to,' she said, icily.

'I could offer you far more. When we get to Herford I'll be rich. I could buy you sparkling jewels to go with your lovely eyes.'

'I don't want to hear any more of this,' she said, turning away.

'I promise to buy you bonnets trimmed with lace,' he called out after her.

His words spurred her to hurry away more quickly. Seeing the result of his offer he began to laugh. He was laughing uproariously as he approached the wagon.

Dora successfully managed to hide her distress from her father when she rejoined her wagon. There was no doubt about it – Hanson was the most horrid man she had ever met.

However, any thoughts about Hanson were

immediately banished when her father revealed a discovery which had come to light while she had been relaxing under the tree.

'The men in the last wagon have dozens of guns.'

'How do you know?' she asked, with alarm.

'One of the young Turvilles, Johnny, saw them. He was playing, chasing some of his brothers, when he tripped and fell as he was going round the last wagon. He held on to the tarpaulin to pull himself up. Part of it came away from the pegs that were holding it. Enough for him to see there were dozens of guns there.'

Dora took in the mental picture in stunned silence. At last she said: 'What are you going to do?'

'What can we do? It's going to take us at least another few days before we reach Herford. All we can do is to carry on as we are. Then, when we get to Herford, we tell the sheriff.'

'Who knows about the guns?'

'The Turville family, of course. And I've told Paul and Harry. All we can hope is that we can keep the gang from finding out that we've discovered their secret.'

'You think they're the gang who robbed the train? The ones that Ben Nolan was chasing?'

'It's pretty obvious, isn't it? There would hardly be two gangs of outlaws with dozens of guns in this part of the world.'

Shortly afterwards the blacksmith announced that he had repaired the wheel.

'Right,' said Sam. 'We've got at least couple of hours of daylight left so we might as well make the most of them.'

'It's hardly worth moving now,' protested one of the wagon drivers.

'The sooner we move, the sooner we'll arrive in Herford,' said Sam.

'I don't see what's the hurry,' grumbled the other, as he prepared to move his wagon.

'I'm afraid I can't tell him,' Sam confided to Dora, as they too took their places in their wagon.

CHAPTER 22

Ben Nolan was making good time. He had been on the road for three days and so far there had been no mishaps. Although the trail between Carlton and Herford was largely unused, from time to time he did come across a rider. He would ask them the same question.

'How far ahead is the wagon train?'

From the answers he received it was obvious he was getting closer. It raised his spirits and helped him to hold on firmly to his resolve to catch it. The question was, would he be in time to stop them before they set off from Herford for the Indian territories?

He had started from Carlton in an unreasoning hurry and after travelling for a few miles he realized that he had made a mistake. He had been so anxious to catch the wagon train that he had omitted to carry out the obvious procedure which, as a trained detective, he should have followed. He should have called in at the sheriff's office in Carlton and acquainted him of his findings, namely that Ossler and his outlaws had driven their wagon towards Carlton, and not away from it as everybody had assumed. If he had spent a little time in the sheriff's office revealing his conviction that Ossler and his outlaws had joined the wagon train it would have achieved two things. One would be that the sheriff could have telegraphed the sheriff of Herford to warn him about the future arrival of the outlaws. The other would be that the sheriff could have telegraphed Pinkerton's in Chicago to inform them that Nolan was going to Herford, chasing the outlaws. He knew that one of the other agents had been sent to Herford at the same time that he had been sent to Carlton. It would be useful if that agent, too, knew about the impending arrival of the wagon train.

But you were in such a hurry to catch up with the wagon train that you omitted these obvious procedures.

All right, I admit I was in a hurry.

To catch the wagon train?

Yes.

You were in a hurry because you wanted to see Dora again.

What's wrong with that? I know she's in danger.

How do you know?

It's as plain as the nose on your face, she's in danger because there are four outlaws travelling on the wagon train who possess forty-eight Winchester rifles. They will stop at nothing to make sure that they get paid for such valuable commodities.

Is that the only reason you dashed out of Carlton?

What are you suggesting?

You can't wait to see Dora again. She's been on your mind ever since the wagon train left Carlton.

All right. I admit it. She's a very attractive young lady.

A headstrong one, I'd say.

All right, a headstrong one as well.

And you'd never forgive yourself if anything happened to her.

You're getting the picture.

Ben was having one of his enforced breaks. Although he found the breaks irksome, he also knew that they were necessary. If he intended to get to Herford in the quickest possible time he knew his priority was to look after his horse – to see that he was regularly fed and had enough water to drink. So every four hours he had a break and, while the horse was grazing, he would eat some of the meagre rations that the saloon keeper's wife had insisted that he take with him. In fact he was eating his last apple and had decided that for the next few days he would have to manage without any food. True, there were plenty of rabbits to be seen and some of them would have been easy to shoot. But shooting a rabbit, skinning it and then cooking it would take up valuable time. Which would delay him in catching up with the wagon train.

How far in front were they? He knew it was no good guessing.

A rider came towards him. Ben hailed him and he pulled up.

'How far ahead is the wagon train?'

'I passed it quite a fair way back,' said the rider. 'They were having trouble with one of the horses. It had lost a shoe. But somebody was fixing it.'

'Thanks,' said Ben. 'By the way, you haven't any spare chow, have you? I'll pay for it.'

'Would a few cans of beans help?'

'It would help me to get to Herford before I die of hunger.'

The rider chuckled as he fished out the cans from his saddle-bag.

CHAPTER 23

'They know we've got guns,' said Ossler.

'How do you know?' demanded Snowy.

'One of the little brats was playing around the wagon. Part of the tarpaulin was loose and he pulled it. He saw the guns.'

'What happened then?' demanded Hanson.

'If you'd been here, where you should have been, instead of making cow's eyes at that young girl, you would have seen what happened next,' snapped Ossler.

'Well, what *did* happen?' asked Filey.

'He told the preacher. Then the preacher told one or two others.'

'It doesn't change anything, does it?' asked Hanson.

'Of course it changes things. If your brains were in your head instead of in your trousers it would be obvious to you.'

'Do we carry on as we had planned?' demanded Filey.

'Of course we do. The preacher and the others are not going to make a move. Especially now they realize we've got enough guns to blow them all to hell, or to heaven. They're just going to sit tight and pretend that they don't know we've got the guns. That is until we arrive in Herford. Then of course they'll head for the sheriff's office.'

'But they'll be too late,' said Snowy.

Ossler favoured him with a grudging smile. 'It's nice to see that one of you has got some sense.'

'When will we be meeting up with the Smith gang?' demanded Filey.

'I sent him a telegram telling him to watch out for the wagon train. As soon as we arrive in Herford we'll join forces.'

'Are there any plans for what we'll do then?' demanded Hanson.

'As you know we've got four dozen rifles. It's obvious we won't need them all.'

'How many are there in Smith's gang?' asked Filey.

'I'm not sure. Six, I think. The same number as we were.'

'When we join together there'll be ten of us,' said Snowy, slowly.

'That's right,' said Ossler. 'So we'll have a lot

of spare guns.'

'What are we going to do with them?'

'It's up to Smith. He knows the situation in Herford. One suggestion is that he could sell them to the Indians.'

'Isn't it dangerous – selling guns to the Indians?' demanded Filey.

'I don't see why,' countered Ossler. 'Other people have been selling guns to the Indians for years.'

'You say we've got thirty-eight guns to sell,' said Snowy. 'They should be worth a great deal of money.'

'They are,' said Ossler, positively.

'Then where are the Indians going to get the money to pay for them? Everybody knows they're poor.'

'Haven't you heard of gold?' replied Ossler. 'There's still gold in the Black Hills, and in other places the Indians know about.'

'I like the idea of having some gold,' said Henson. 'I could have some made into a ring. It would help to impress the young ladies.'

'Talking about impressing the ladies, you keep away from the preacher's daughter,' said Ossler. 'I saw you trying to seduce her when the two of you were sheltering under the tree.'

'It was only a bit of fun,' said Hanson, defensively.

'We know about your "bits of fun" in the past, and the trouble they've got us into.'

'There was that farmer's daughter,' stated Filey. 'We camped on his land and we could have stayed there for as long as we liked. But you had to seduce his daughter in the hayloft and we all had to leave in a hurry.'

'I can't help it if I'm attracted to the fair sex.'

'You should take up a less dangerous occupation,' said Filey. 'Like gambling.'

'What about the last time you lost hundreds of dollars at cards,' said Hanson. 'When you couldn't pay up the other guy threatened to shoot you. It was only because we happened to be in the saloon and shot him first that you're alive today.'

'That was a misunderstanding,' said Filey.

'Some misunderstanding,' said Snowy. 'You were hoping to win the jackpot with a pair of kings. While the other guy had a full house.'

'To come back to the present,' said Ossler. 'There's one thing we've got to watch out for.'

'What's that?' demanded Hanson.

'If we're overtaken on the road, say by a cowboy, we've got to make sure that the preacher doesn't get a message to him. He could try to get a message to somebody to take it to the sheriff in Herford. Then when we get there we'll find we have a warm reception.'

124

'We'll keep our eyes peeled,' promised Filey.

'I wonder what the Indian squaws are like,' said Hanson, thoughtfully.

CHAPTER 24

In a tepee a few miles to the north of Herford a meeting was taking place. It was unusual in that of the four in the tent, two were Indians and two were white men.

The Indian, who was named Running Grass, spoke.

'You say you have rifles?'

'Yes,' replied Roland Smith, 'We've got rifles.'

'New rifles,' added his companion, Craig Tindall.

'How many?' asked the other Indian, named Old In The Head.

'Thirty-six,' replied Smith.

Running Grass looked puzzled The other Indian held up his two hands three times to signify thirty, then held up six fingers.

'You'd like to sell them?' asked Running Grass.

'You'd like to buy?' demanded Smith. He could see that he held the interest of the Indians with his proposition.

'We haven't any money.' Running Grass spread out his hands to emphasize the point.

'We've heard that you've got gold,' said Tindall.

'Ah, gold!' Old In The Head nodded.

'You pay us in gold instead of money,' said Smith.

'First we must see the guns,' said Running Grass.

'They will be arriving in Herford any day now. They're coming in on a wagon train.'

'We must see the gold,' said Tindall.

For answer Running Grass reached into a pouch he was wearing round his waist. He pulled out a piece of metal that gleamed even in the poor light of the tepee. He handed it to Smith. Smith examined it and in turn passed it onto Tindall, who, having held the nugget in his hands for a few seconds, passed it back to the Indian.

'That gold buy many guns,' stated Old In The Head.

'We'd have to see whether this is real gold and not fool's gold,' said Smith.

'How will you know?' demanded Old In The Head.

'We will take it to the bank. They are used to dealing in gold. They will tell us how many dollars this is worth.'

Running Grass nodded. 'You take Old In The Head with you. You will find out how many guns this nugget will buy. If you need more we can arrange it.'

The three left. Their horses were grazing outside the tepee. The three mounted and set off towards Herford.

Half an hour later they entered the bank. Smith explained to the cashier that they wanted some gold assayed. The cashier informed them that Mr Morris dealt with the gold. A few minutes later they were seated in his office.

Mr Morris examined the gold critically, first by holding it in his hand and then from several angles under a small microscope. Finally he weighed it. The examination took several minutes and Smith became impatient. Old In The Head sat utterly immobile.

'Well?' demanded Smith.

'It's pure gold,' announced Morris.

'How much is it worth?' demanded Tindall.

'If you wished to sell it to the bank I could give you sixty dollars for it.'

'I thought we'd get more than that,' said a disappointed Smith.

'It's the market price. Since we've been getting the gold coming in from the Black Hills, the price has come down.'

Tindall thanked him and they left the bank.

'Is what the man in bank said bad news?' enquired Old In The Head.

'It means we'll have to have a lot of nuggets to pay for the guns,' Smith explained.

'That's no problem. We can get from the cave.'

The two outlaws, whose interest in the transaction involving the guns had cooled when they realized that the nugget wasn't worth as much as they had thought, evinced sudden interest at the mention of the cave.

'You can get a lot more nuggets like that?' enquired Smith.

'Lots.' The Indian indicated on his fingers at least fifty nuggets.

'That will pay for the guns,' said Smith, excitedly.

'When will we see the guns?' demanded the Indian.

'Two or three days. The guns are in a wagon on its way from Carlton. The wagon is part of a wagon train.'

'How long will it take you to get the gold

nuggets?' demanded Tindall.

'Two or three days,' replied Old In The Head. 'We will meet in the tepee in three days' time.'

'It's a deal,' said a delighted Smith.

CHAPTER 25

The next event to slow the wagon train's progress occurred when they became aware that another horse-drawn vehicle was following them – it was the stagecoach from Carlton to Herford. Normally the driver of the stage kept his six horses moving at a gallop. He had a schedule to keep to and it was a source of pride to him to keep to it if he could. Heavy rains and other adverse conditions such as fallen rocks could hinder and slow his progress from time to time, but when the weather was fine, as it had been for the past few weeks, he expected to make good progress.

The wagon train drivers, having become aware of the stagecoach following them, brought their wagons to a halt. The stagecoach driver, when he spied the wagon train ahead, pulled on the horses' reins and brought then to a gradual halt. The people in the stage peered out through the windows at the wagons.

'All right,' said the driver. 'You can all have time to stretch your legs and the gentlemen can have a smoke.'

The half a dozen passengers happily disembarked. They began to mingle with the folk from the wagons who had come out to greet them.

'Why are we stopping?' demanded Snowy, from inside the wagon.

'The stage has caught up with us,' said Ossler. 'I want you and Hanson to come with me. You, Filey, stay here. And make sure nobody comes snooping around.'

Sam and Dora, being in the front wagon, were strolling to meet the stagecoach passengers when they were accosted by the three outlaws.

'What do you want?' demanded Sam.

'We just want to make sure that you don't speak out of turn when you talk to the stage driver,' said Ossler.

'I don't know what you mean,' said Sam.

'Oh, I think you do. You know that we've got guns in our wagon. If you breathe a word about it to anyone on the stage, it would be very unwise.'

'It would be very unwise,' echoed Hanson, who had taken up a position behind Dora and now grabbed her arm.

Dora gave a startled gasp. Since the others on the wagon train had gone ahead to greet the stage passengers, nobody took any notice of the slight noise.

'I want you to pass the message to your two friends who also know about our guns,' said Ossler. 'Filey will come with you to see that you don't try any tricks.'

'If you do, you will find that your daughter will have a nasty scar down her face.' Hanson emphasized the point by drawing a small knife and holding it to Dora's cheek.

'Don't harm her,' cried Sam.

'Just give that lot a few minutes and then tell them we want to be moving,' said Ossler. 'We don't want them having any long discussions.'

'Keep everything short,' said Hanson. 'Beauty here stays with us as a guarantee that you don't try any tricks.'

With a last despairing glance behind him Sam went ahead to catch up his two friends. Dora was left in Hanson's grasp. He moved her forcibly until they were behind one of the wagons and out of sight of the others.

'Take your filthy hands off me,' gasped Dora, as she struggled to pull his hands away.

Hanson was considerably stronger than she was and had managed to pin her against one of the wagons, so restricting her movements.

'Remember yesterday when you were sheltering under the tree?'

'What about it?' She turned her head away from his face. She could smell the whiskey on his breath.

'I said I wanted a bit of fun.' As he spoke his head came nearer to hers. The smell of whiskey was overpowering. She closed her eyes. 'I think we'll start with a kiss.'

Hanson turned her head so that she was facing him. Then he kissed her fiercely on the lips. When they eventually drew apart he said: 'That was worth waiting for.'

Dora's reply was to spit in his face.

'Well, well,' sneered Hanson. 'The things they teach you Christians these days.'

'Let me go,' Dora half sobbed.

'Not until you've paid for spitting at me.'

This time he began to fondle her breasts as he kissed her again.

Why was this happening to her? She had been brought up as a good Christian. She had always tried to help others if she could. She had always tried to see the best side of people's natures. But now this beast was pawing her. It was enough to make a person lose faith the in the goodness of God.

His hands were now fumbling between her

skirts. In order to achieve his object he had put his knife on the ledge at the back of the wagon. Dora shifted her position so that she would be able to reach it.

Hanson gave a grunt of satisfaction as he achieved his goal. At the same time she grabbed the knife and held it against his throat.

'If you don't leave me alone I'll slit your throat like the pig you are,' Dora hissed.

It took Hanson two seconds to be convinced that she meant what she said. He reluctantly let her go.

He was panting with frustration as she held the knife pointing at him. The other travellers were beginning to drift back from their meeting with the people in the stage.

'I haven't finished with you yet, beauty,' snarled Hanson. 'We've got three days to go before we reach Carlton. It will give me plenty of time to finish off what we had started.'

Dora's reply was to fling his knife to the ground. She watched him, white-faced, as he picked it up and walked away.

CHAPTER 26

In Fort Willoughby Major Hawkins was seated at his desk as usual. What was unusual was that he had called his two captains to his office so early in the morning. The two, Blinton and Drydale, were seated opposite him, waiting for him to announce the reason for the early-morning meeting.

'Right, gentlemen.' The major looked up from a dispatch he had been reading. 'I'm not going to conceal from you the seriousness of the situation.'

They waited for his announcement about just how serious the situation was. Both were in their late twenties, but while Blinton was married and his wife was living on the fort, Drydale was still enjoying the life of a bachelor.

'We have proof here,' the major tapped the dispatch, 'that the Indians are on the warpath

136

again. More specifically, the Lakota Sioux.'

'That is bad news, sir,' said Blinton.

'I thought, since the last Indian wars, everything was under control,' said Drydale.

'So did we,' said the major. 'But according to my information the Lakota Sioux have been forming war parties. They've been doing the ghost dance.'

'What exactly is the ghost dance?' demanded Bunton.

'They dance in a circle for hours on end – sometimes even days,' stated Drydale. 'They think it bestows on them invincible powers.'

'If – as you say – the Indians are on the warpath, sir,' said Blinton, 'where are they going to get their armaments from? Surely they're not just going to depend on their bows and arrows.'

'That's a good question, Blinton,' replied the major. 'According to our information they haven't yet got hold of rifles, but they are in the process of doing so.'

'Where are they going to get them from?' demanded Drydale.

'From a wagon train.'

Both men looked puzzled by their superior officer's announcement.

The major permitted himself a slight smile at their expressions.

'It's like this,' he continued. 'The sheriff of

Herford has received a telegram from the sheriff of Carlton saying that forty-eight Winchester rifles and ammunition are on the wagon train which is now on its way from Carlton to Herford. He received the information a few days ago from a feller named Grizzly Smalls. The information was passed on to headquarters, but only now have they passed it on to us.'

'I know Grizzly Smalls,' said Drydale. 'I've often met him in a saloon. He used to be an Indian scout.'

Blinton frowned at his fellow officer's recollection of his drinking habits. He himself was a teetotaller, and believed that his fellow officers should observe the same abstinence.

'I've heard of him, too,' said the major. 'Although I've never been in his company. The point is that I think we can treat any information he has passed on to us as accurate.'

'I'm sure we can,' Drydale confirmed with a nod.

'Do we know when this wagon train is supposed to arrive in Herford?' asked Blinton.

'We can only make a rough estimate. It left Carlton six days ago. It should take nine or ten days to reach Herford. As far as we can tell it should reach Herford in about two days' time.'

'And you want us to intercept the guns,' stated Drydale.

'I know it's a lot to ask. We're about thirty miles from Herford. If we can get at the guns before the Indians we could save a considerable amount of bloodshed. A considerable amount,' he emphasized.

'I suppose we'll have to go to Herford in the first place to check with the sheriff to see whether the wagon train has arrived there. Then take the trail to Carlton,' said Drydale.

'That's exactly what you'll have to do. I'll want the men ready on their horses in an hour's time. It's imperative to move quickly.'

'How many men do you want us to take, sir?' asked Blinton.

'As you know, the fort is understaffed at the moment. All I can spare is thirty.'

He dismissed the two officers. When they were walking towards their billets Blinton said: 'Let's hope we can get to the guns before the Indians do.'

'Oh, I don't know,' said Drydale. 'If we have a good old shoot-out it will add some excitement to this dull life.'

'Some excitement if you're in danger of getting killed!' said Blinton, scornfully.

CHAPTER 27

Tom Milton, sheriff of Herford, was a worried man. His expression told his deputy, Frank Gardner, more than any words could about the present sate of Milton's mind.

'Perhaps you'd better go and check again,' the sheriff said.

'But I only went outside ten minutes ago,' protested Gardner.

The sheriff glanced up at the clock on the wall. 'But the stage should have arrived by now. Sandy is hardly ever late.'

'Maybe this is the one occasion when he is late for some reason or other,' suggested Gardner.

'Go and check,' commanded the sheriff, in tones which brooked no argument.

Gardner went outside. Their office was on the main square in Herford. It could not have been more centrally situated. When the stage pulled in it invariably stopped about a hundred yards away. The driver, nicknamed Sandy because of the colour of his hair, would bring any letters to their office while the passengers were disembarking. But, as the sheriff said, so far there was no sign of him.

Of course he knew why the sheriff was on pins. It wasn't the late arrival of the stage that concerned him – but whether the stage had passed the wagon train on its way. If it had then they wanted to know how far the wagon train was from Herford.

Ever since they had received the telegram from the sheriff of Carlton their normal peaceful mode of life had changed. The sheriff had immediately dispatched a telegram to army headquarters warning them that about the guns. That was five days ago. On the assumption that it would take the Ninth Cavalry two days to arrive in Herford they should have been here three days ago. But so far there no sign of them. At first every day that passed, and now every hour, meant that the town was in danger of being invaded by outlaws who had dozens of rifles at their disposal.

Dan Jackson, who had a whiskey-stall at the other end of the square, came across.

'Waiting for the stage, Frank?' asked Dan.

'It's late,' said Frank, automatically looking at his watch.

141

'I know. The sooner it comes, the sooner I can get rid of some of my bottles. That's one thing about a stage journey: the travellers always arrive thirsty.'

Frank managed a smile. 'We've got more important things to think about than the passengers' thirst.'

'Something important on the stage?' Dan was always alive for a morsel of gossip. In the first place he liked to keep in touch with what was going on in Herford. And in the second place his daughter, Daisy, liked to keep up with the latest gossip.

'It's not something that's on the stage. It's what's on the wagon train that concerns us.'

He explained to a puzzled Dan about the guns on the wagon train.

'You think the stage would have overtaken the wagon train?'

'It's bound to. A wagon train doesn't travel all that quickly as you know.'

'What about those guns?' A worried frown was beginning to show on Dan's forehead.

'They are rifles which were stolen from a train outside Carlton a couple of weeks ago.'

'I read about that. So if the outlaws who stole the guns are coming here on the wagon train that means there could be trouble here.'

'Exactly. That's why we've sent for the Cavalry.'

Daisy joined them. She was a pretty twenty-one-year-old.

'There could be trouble here,' her father explained. 'Some outlaws are bringing rifles into the town.'

'We've sent for the Cavalry,' explained Frank 'We're hoping they get here before the outlaws, so that they can defend the town.'

'They can defend me anytime they like,' said Daisy. 'Think of it, all those young men in their soldier's uniforms.'

While the conversation was going on Frank kept glancing in the direction from which the stage would come.

'What do you think I'd better do about my stall?' asked Dan.

'If I were you, I'd take it down,' replied Frank. 'There could be some shooting.'

CHAPTER 28

The deputy sheriff's words were prophetic but the shooting was taking place several miles to the south of the town. Having returned to their wagons the travellers showed a new-found urgency in getting their wagons moving. Several of them had asked the stage driver how far away they were from Herford. When he had informed them that they had about ten miles to go, and there was a chance they would make it before sunset, it galvanized them into moving quickly.

Sam was pleased with this new-found urgency as he gave the familiar shout, 'Wagons roll'. His one regret was that he hadn't been able to pass on the message to the stage driver about the outlaws. It would have been perfect if he had informed the driver about the guns, then presumably the sheriff would be prepared to anticipate the arrival of the outlaws. As it stood when they arrived in Herford the element of surprise would be with the outlaws. Ah, well, it was out of his hands now. His main concern was to get the wagon to Herford before sundown.

Dora, too, was busy with her own thoughts. They were unpleasant ones which refused to go away. Her confrontation with Hanson would stay with her for a long time. She could still taste the sickening smell of whiskey on his breath when he had kissed her. She could still feel him crushing her against the wagon when he had pawed her. She knew from reading reports in the newspapers that such scum existed. Yes, scum was the right word for them. Her father had always taught her to try to see the good side of anybody's nature. Someone is never wholly bad, he had often preached in his pulpit. But as far as she was concerned men like Hanson didn't deserve to be in a civilized society.

They were both too occupied with their thoughts to look around at the scenery through which they were travelling. If they had they would have noticed that it consisted of low hills. Also, if they had been very observant, they might have spotted a few Indians who were riding parallel to the wagon train.

'That must be it,' said Running Grass.

'There wouldn't be two wagon trains going to Herford,' said Old In The Head.

145

'The outlaw thought we were going to do a deal with him to get the rifles,' said Running Grass.

'Why should we do a deal when we can help ourselves to the rifles?' said the other.

'They're not travelling very fast.'

'That will make it easier when we attack them. The question is, which wagon is the one with the rifles in it?'

'We'll find out soon enough when we attack and they start firing at us with rifles.'

'Yes, but we want to attack before they start firing at us with rifles. That way none of us will get killed,' said Old In The Head.

They had been studying the nine wagons while they kept them in sight.

'The rifles could be in any one of the wagons,' observed Running Grass.

'I think I know which one they're in.'

'Which one?' demanded Running Grass excitedly.

'The last one.'

'Why do you say that?'

'If you look at the wagons they're all the same except the last one.'

'I see what you mean,' said the other, slowly. 'All the other wagons have opened their covers, except the last one.'

'Exactly. The last one is closed up because the

146

rifles are in it.'

'I hope you're right,' said Running Grass.

He called the war party together. He explained to them exactly what they must do when he gave the signal.

'We had better attack soon,' said Old In The Head. 'We don't want to get too near Herford.'

The others nodded in agreement.

The first hint the travellers in the wagon train had that something was about to happen was when they saw a couple of dozen Indians, with their bodies painted red, galloping towards them. They hardly had time to grasp the significance of the scene before the first casualty was claimed. Filey was the driver of the last wagon. The Indians came down from a low hill to their left and for a second he thought his eyes had deceived him when he saw them charging towards him. Too late he realized that they were Indians on the war path. Running Grass's arrow hit him in the chest and a second later he toppled from the driver's seat.

Pandemonium had broken out among the travellers, who had seen the approaching Indians. Some of the men possessed guns but they were almost all stored away in the wagons, on the assumption that they wouldn't be used on the journey to Herford. Women and children were screaming at the frightening sight of the

Indians with their painted bodies. Snowy's head emerged from their wagon to see what all the excitement was about. It was his last move on earth as Old In The Head's arrow struck him accurately in the chest.

'We're being attacked by Indians,' shouted Ossler.

In fact two of the Indians had already jumped up on to the wagon. The weapons which could have been used to ward off the attack were lying in their boxes out of reach. Also, neither Ossler nor Hanson were carrying revolvers, assuming that their journey to Herford would be a peaceful one. They were allowed no time to regret their decision since one Indian was on to Hanson in a flash and drove his knife into his heart. The other Indian tried to dispatch Ossler in a similar manner, but Ossler was nearer the tail-gate of the wagon. He hurled himself over it and started to race towards the next wagon. He had almost reached it when an Indian threw a tomahawk at the running figure. His aim was accurate, the weapon almost slicing Ossler's head in half.

Panic had rapidly spread through the wagon train. When those near the rear wagon saw the way the Indians had dispatched the outlaws the panic took different forms. Some tried to hide by diving back inside their wagons. Some ran for the nearby grass verges, hoping to find shelter among the trees, some even fell on their knees and began to pray, firmly believing that the end of their lives was near. There were women screaming as they tried to shelter their children from the terrible sights they had witnessed A few of their menfolk had gone back inside their wagons and seized hold of the guns they had brought with them. These had been intended for shooting rabbits and wild pigs, but now the men intended using them to defend their families.

The battle between the few who tried to defend themselves in that way was so one-sided that it was over on a few minutes. The Indians were circling round the wagons uttering their blood-curdling war cry. They were riding so quickly that the men with their guns were unable to get good shots at them. The result was that three of the wagon-owners ended up with arrows in their chests while only one of the Indians was injured by a bullet.

The fact that some of the men in the wagon train had fired at them drove Running Grass to a new course of action. Until then he had been content to drive away with the wagon containing the guns and leave the rest of the wagon-owners alone. But seeing the result of the skirmish changed his mind. He called on a group of

Indians he had so far kept in reserve. They had bows and arrows like the others. The difference was that there was dried grass attached to the arrows. Running Grass gave a command and the Indians proceeded to light the arrows.

In the front of the wagon train Sam and Dora had watched helplessly while the outlaws had been killed. Sam had even started to move towards the back of the wagon but Dora gripped his arm fiercely.

'Let them kill them, they're only outlaws.'

'They're all God's creatures.'

However Sam let himself be persuaded not to go to the back of the wagon train. Dora also held on to him tightly when the three men tried to defend their wagons. In fact Sam wouldn't have been able to use any arms against the Indians since he didn't carry any – being a firm believer that peace in the end will prevail over war. However when he saw the Indians advancing with their lighted arrows and realized the sickening horror of their intentions he shrugged away Dora's grasp. He advanced towards the Indians.

'Leave our wagons alone,' he cried. 'You've got your guns, go away and leave us in peace. We can't harm you now – we haven't any weapons. I'm a man of peace, but if you burn our wagons I swear I will pray for the destruction of all of you. If you burn our wagons may you all burn in hell as retribution. When I hear that you have all been killed by the soldiers, which I prophesy will be your end, I will rejoice and give thanks to the Lord.'

The preacher had given many speeches in the pulpit in his life but never one with so much passion as he delivered this one. It left Old In The Head unimpressed. He gave a signal to the Indians with the fire arrows. They proceeded to shoot them into the wagons.

However the Indians were not entirely finished with the wagon train. Running Grass took careful aim at Sam as he stood facing the Indians with the fire arrows. Running Grass's arrow unerringly found Sam's heart.

CHAPTER 29

The acrid smell of burning reached Ben as he rode quickly in the direction of Herford. He was puzzled by the way it pervaded the atmosphere. The only conclusion he could arrive at was that somebody, somewhere, was burning a huge fire.

But fires were not common in that part of the world. For one thing the grass was too short for anyone to be able to collect enough together to make a sizable fire. True, there were trees dotted around here and there. But it would require a considerable amount of effort to chop down a whole tree to build a fire which would fill the sky with smoke as this one was in the process of doing.

Of course, nearer the towns there were farms. They were in the habit of burning unwanted farm produce. But he must be too far away from Herford and therefore too far away from any farm which would be burning the quantity of farm refuse that would be needed to make this amount of smoke.

Suddenly he was struck by a terrible thought. What was one of the most combustible things he knew? A wagon. The smoke could be coming from a wagon burning. Or, even worse, several wagons. He spurred his horse in a mad gallop to reach the fire.

The smoke grew thicker as he sped along the trail. It was billowing in clouds which grew darker. There was a bend in the trail ahead but he could hardly see it until he had almost reached it. When he did turn the corner he was met by a heartbreaking sight.

The wagons which had started off so proudly several days ago now were burnt-out shells. There was something pathetic about their appearance – an impression which was heightened by the fact that the horses had been taken from among the shafts. Some of the travellers had tried to save their belongings by carrying them on to the side of the trail, which looked like a graveyard with all the packing cases, beds, tables and chairs scattered around randomly.

There were people sitting around – invariably with expressions of hopelessness on their faces. Some of them glanced up when they saw Ben approach. Others, convinced that they had lost everything, did not even bother to glance at him.

Panic gripped him when he realized that there was no sign of Dora. He scanned the faces desperately as he rode by the side of the wagons. He recognized the faces of Harry and Paul as he passed. Instead of giving him a wave of recognition they too stared at him with the same expression of hopelessness as was on the faces of the others.

Suddenly, to his indescribable relief there she was. She was standing by the side of the front wagon. Like the others, it too, was a burnt-out shell. When he approached she glanced up at him. Her face wore the saddest expression he had ever come across.

'He's dead.' She pointed to what was obviously a figure on the ground completely covered by a blanket.

'Your father?'

She nodded.

'What happened?'

'Indians came. They shot the outlaws and took the guns. They had arrows with them to start a fire. Dad pleaded with them to spare the wagons. They shot him.'

'The bastards.'

'If I had a gun I'd go after them and shoot every one of them,' she said viciously.

'How many more did the Indians kill?'

'I think there are two others. They went to get their guns to try to defend their wagons. The Indians shot them.'

Harry and Paul approached them.

'The Indians took the horses,' said Paul.

'There are three dead outlaws in the last wagon,' said Harry. 'One of them is still alive though. He said something that doesn't make sense to me. He said that the Smith gang must have done a deal with the Indians.'

'It makes sense to me,' said Ben, grimly.

'What are we going to do?' demanded Harry. 'We can't move from here.'

'How far is it to Herford?' demanded Ben.

'I'd guess about six miles,' said Paul.

'Right. You come with me,' Ben said to Dora.

'I can't leave him,' she cried, moving towards her father's body.

'You've got to,' said Ben. 'You've got to come to Herford to arrange the funerals.'

'Can't you do it?' she pleaded.

'I haven't got time. I've got to see the sheriff about catching the Smith gang.'

'What about the Indians?' demanded Paul.

'That'll be up to the army. They'll have to send for the cavalry to take on the Indians.'

Dora, seeing there was no choice but to accompany Ben, knelt down by her father. She gently lifted a corner of the makeshift shroud and kissed his face. When she put the cover back there were tears in her eyes.

'Come on,' said Ben, gruffly. 'There's work to be done.'

He mounted his horse and she obediently jumped up behind.

'Hold on,' he said, as they began to ride towards Herford.

Half an hour later they were riding down Main Street. Ben had been to Herford on one occasion before and knew that the sheriff's office was on the square. When they arrived there he jumped down and helped Dora down.

'I'll see you here later,' he told her. He hurried into the sheriff's office.

'What can I do for you?' demanded the sheriff.

It took Ben a few minutes to explain who he was and what had happened to the wagon train a few miles out of the town.

'We were expecting the wagon train. The stagecoach driver told us that he had passed it a few miles back.'

'Well, it's still there,' snapped Ben.

'What do you know about the Smith gang?' demanded the sheriff.

'Not much. If I remember rightly the leader's name is Roland Smith.'

'Here he is,' said the deputy, excitedly. He had been searching through the pictures on the wall. 'That's him.' He pointed to a drawing of a clean-shaven man with an unremarkable face.

'The chances are he's still in town,' said Ben.

At that moment Dan knocked and entered.

'Have you any news about the rifles?' he demanded.

The deputy introduced the newcomer as the town's chief supplier of whiskey.

'The Indians have got the rifles and they're on their way back to their territory,' said Ben.

'Do you know this guy?' the deputy asked Dan, pointing to the drawing of Smith.

'Sure,' said Dan. 'He and some of his friends wanted to buy a few bottles of my whiskey an hour or so ago. I only let them have one bottle because I wanted to keep a few bottles for the folks on the stage.'

'You wouldn't know where they went after they bought the whiskey?' demanded the sheriff.

'Sure. They went across to the Buffalo's Head.'

'Dan, you're a genius,' said the deputy, excitedly.

'Wait a minute,' said Ben, as Dan was about to leave. 'Did you notice how many men there were?'

'I'm not sure.' Dan scratched his head. 'About

five or six, I reckon.'

'Let's say there are six,' said the sheriff, as he proceeded to take a rifle down from the rack and handed it to his deputy. 'And there are two of us.'

'You can make that three,' stated Ben.

The Buffalo's Head was on the far corner of the square. Some of the bystanders stared in surprise as the three grim-faced men marched towards it.

When they reached the entrance to the saloon the sheriff said: 'We're going to do this according to the law. I'm going to challenge them to drop their gunbelts. If they don't then you two are free to start shooting.'

The sheriff didn't have to challenge Smith and his outlaws. When they saw the sheriff and his deputy enter they instinctively went for their guns. Ben had drawn his revolver before going into the saloon. He spotted Smith, recognizable from the picture in the sheriff's office. This was the person who had been responsible for selling the guns to the Indians – and so was responsible for the destruction of the wagon train and the killing of Dora's father. There was naked hatred in Ben's face as he pumped bullets into the outlaw.

To Ben's right and left the two rifles were also dealing out death. There were soon four bodies lying on the floor. One of the remaining two outlaws was facing Ben. He had drawn his revolver and Ben prepared to dispatch him in the same way as he had dispatched his boss. To his horror Ben discovered from the click of his revolver that he had emptied the chamber into Smith. The outlaw's face split into a wolflike smile as he realized he had Ben at his mercy. He even hesitated for a second in order to let Ben know that he was about to die. There was no way he could be saved, for the deputy and sheriff were at the far end of the bar and they couldn't get involved in the gunfight since Ben was directly in their line of fire.

To the outlaw's surprise Ben dropped on one knee. The outlaw hesitated and adjusted his aim to shoot the kneeling figure. However the bullet never left his revolver. In a movement that was so quick the eye could hardly follow it Ben had produced a knife from his boot and sent it unerringly into the outlaw's heart.

'That was a good move,' said the deputy admiringly.

'It's an old circus trick,' said Ben, with more than a little relief in his voice.

The remaining outlaw surrendered without a fight.

The annals of the Indian wars relate how the Indians were on their way back to their territory when to their surprise they found a detachment of the Ninth Cavalry riding towards them. The precious rifles with which the Indians hoped to start another uprising were in the wagon and they had no time to use them. A bloody battle ensued but there was bound to be only one conclusion – the soldier's rifles proving the winners. One last battle between the Indians and the cavalry took place a couple of years later – known as the Battle of Wounded Knee. Again the Indians were annihilated. Not that it made any difference to Ben and Dora who were back living in Carlton. Dora was expecting her second child and her husband had accepted the position of sheriff when the incumbent's weight had finally proved to be too much of a problem. Ben never did explain to Dora how close he had been to death, when in a moment of blind anger he failed to count the number of bullets he pumped into the outlaw in Herford.